THE FAMILY TRAP

Accident
After the Wedding
The Amazing Miss Laura
Bride at Eighteen
Ellie's Inheritance
The Happenings at North End School
Rachel's Legacy
Sometimes I Don't Love My Mother

Hila Colman

THE FAMILY TRAP

TRAP

William Morrow and Company
New York 1982

Printed in the United States of America.
1   2   3   4   5   6   7   8   9   10

Library of Congress Cataloging in Publication Data

Colman, Hila.
  The family trap.
  Summary: With her father dead and her mother in a mental institu-tion, sixteen-year-old Becky, chafing under the authority of her older sis-ter, petitions the juvenile court to become an emancipated minor.
  [1. Brothers and sisters—Fiction.   2. Family problems—Fiction]
I. Title.
PZ7.C7Fan   1982   [Fic]   82-12495
ISBN 0-688-01472-0

THE FAMILY TRAP

1

It was April when they stood together in a gloomy room while the young doctor talked to them. The afternoon sun filtering through the high, small-frame windows cast shadows across the dark paneled room instead of brightening it. Becky Jones stood slightly behind her sister Nancy, who, as the oldest, was the one the doctor was addressing. Little Stacey held a tight grip on Becky's hand. All three were listening quietly. Becky could hear everything the bearded man in the white coat was saying, yet her mind was elsewhere.

"We think we can help your mother here, but we can't make any promises. I cannot say that she will be well in two months, six months, or a year. Or if she will ever be well enough to function normally. I wish I could." His earnest face broke into an apologetic smile. "We'll do our best, but we are not miracle workers."

"No, of course not," Nancy murmured. "But if you could give us some idea . . . " Her voice trailed off uncertainly.

"I can't," he said flatly. "I'm sorry." Becky tugged at Nancy's sleeve. She knew he was dismissing them. She wanted to get out of there anyway. She didn't need him to tell them that their mother was very, very sick. There had been no mistaking the look of fear on Mrs. Jones's white, tense face when she had said good-bye and the nurse had taken her away crying. They had long, fancy names for her mother's mental breakdown, but Becky knew her mother was not so crazy that she didn't know she was saying good-bye to her daughters for a long time.

Becky glanced at her sisters uneasily. It was going to be the three of them now, and the prospect was not consoling. There had been times when the thought of living without parents had sounded exciting: no one to tell you what to do, when to come home, or to fuss about your homework. But since her father's accident and her mother's illness, Becky had had a taste of it, and she didn't like it. Besides, there was Nancy. Her sister was there with her quick assumption that she was in charge and had to play mother and father, acting as if God had appointed her to make them a family again and her the head of it. But Nancy was not wise and fun like their father had been nor soft and endearing like their mother. Nancy was Nancy, okay as a sister, sometimes a pain, sometimes lovable, but definitely not someone you wanted as your self-appointed parent.

All the while the doctor was talking and Becky's mind was wandering, her mother's unhappy face was before her. She almost wished her mother had been robbed of all awareness, that she had been left empty and silly like some of the patients they had glimpsed strolling on the lawns outside. But her mother knew. Mrs. Jones remembered little things like telling Stacey to be sure to put the rubber bands on her teeth at night, telling Becky that when she vacuumed her room she had to get under the bed; and to Nancy . . . Becky turned away to hide her tears.

"I'm no good," their mother had said. "I'm a failure. I wasn't a good wife, I'm not a good mother, I should be dead. They should have let me die. I shouldn't be here, taking up space. . . ." The nurse had taken her away when she had begun to cry hysterically. "Don't worry," Nancy had called as she ran after them. "I'll take care of the girls. I'll be a good mother." She'd had a bright smile on her face although her cheeks were wet.

Their mother blamed herself for everything: for the accident that killed their father, for the way she had botched her attempted suicide, for Stacey's crooked teeth, for Becky's straight hair, for rain, for dry spells, for flowers that died, and for mice in the basement. There wasn't anything in the world that wasn't her fault—even nuclear weapons and stabbings thousands of miles away.

Her mother's overwhelming feelings of guilt frightened Becky. She thought of asking the doctor if it could be inherited, but she knew it was a silly question. But still she felt her own guilt in wishing Nancy wasn't so eager to take their mother's place.

They said good-bye to the doctor and Becky tried to hurry them out. She wanted to get into the fresh air, away from the hospital smell of disinfectant and unhappiness. After last night's rain the mushrooms up on their hillside would be out in full force and for a moment Becky let her mind linger on happier days when her father used to take her out and they would pick whole baskets full.

But how could she be thinking of herself and mushrooms when they were leaving their mother in this huge, cold, frightening place?

The social worker in the hospital had said they had to go on with their lives as before. She was a tall, dark-skinned woman who looked forbidding before she began to talk. But her voice and smile were warm, and she had impulsively given Stacey a kiss before they left her tiny office. "Your mother is going to be well taken care of here," she had said. "We will do everything to make her comfortable. But don't be upset if you are asked not to come see her. Sometimes a patient gets too emotionally upset by visitors who are close and loved. You will have to let her doctor decide when you can visit."

"Yes, of course," Nancy had murmured, but Becky was annoyed. She had wanted to ask, "How will the doctor know if seeing us may not be exactly what she wants and needs?" Suddenly she had felt overwhelmed by what was happening: They were leaving their mother with strangers who were going to make cold, analytical decisions about what was right without really knowing the kind of family they were. No one had asked the proper questions about what they had been like before all the terrible things had happened. They weren't a sad-sack, scared group who spent time in hospitals and had interviews with social workers who felt sorry for them. Becky had never been in a hospital in her life before her father's accident, except for the time she had gone to see her friend Lisa, who had broken her leg.

Becky had wanted to tell the soft-spoken social worker, "You don't understand. We're not like other families. We *care* about each other. We're not like most kids who don't get along with their parents; we always had a good time with them. Sometimes Nancy and I have fights, but they're not serious either. My mother won't understand if we don't come to see her." But the social worker had had a telephone call, and had held the phone aside for a few seconds while she said good-bye to them hurriedly and bestowed her kiss on Stacey.

Now they left the doctor's office. Becky saw him, too, pick up his telephone and figured that in about a minute he would be on to someone else and forget all about them too. Silently they walked across the parking lot to their car.

"We can stop and do some marketing on our way home," Nancy said as she slid behind the wheel of their father's old station wagon.

"No, let's go home," Becky said. She was sitting next to Nancy; Stacey was in the back.

"Can I get some ice cream?" Stacey asked.

"You'll have supper when you get home," Nancy said to Stacey. She sounded like a mother, but not soft-voiced like theirs. "You can't have ice cream just before you eat."

"Mommy would have let me."

Becky gave Nancy a swift glance. Mommy, Mommy . . . their lives could not go on the same. Everything was going to be different. Becky turned around and patted Stacey. Nancy stepped on the brake for a caution light.

"You could have gone ahead. It's not red yet," Becky said.

"Don't be a backseat driver."

"She's not in the back, she's in front," Stacey contributed.

"Do you have to shop now?" Becky asked. She wanted to be home, alone in her room with her thoughts. The market, and meeting people she knew, would be unbearable. Becky glanced at Nancy's stern face, then turned away and stared through the window.

Nancy took one look at her and pulled the car to the side of the road. "If you want to cry, go ahead," she said.

Tears glistened in Becky's eyes. "What do you think I am, one of those dolls who cries on order?"

"I just thought . . . "

"Don't think. Don't . . . " And then she burst into sobs. She ran out of the car and sat down on the ground with her head in her arms. In a few minutes she was climbing back into the car, laughing with the tears wetting her face. "This is cuckoo. Like stopping on the road to pee in the bushes. Come on, let's go."

Nancy shook her head, helpless in the face of her younger sister's quick change of mood. "I'm not going to be able to handle you."

"Then don't. Don't even try. I don't need to be handled."

Nancy was silent until she pulled the car into the market parking area and turned off the motor. She turned to Becky and said quietly, "Let's not quarrel. Everything is awful enough."

Becky sat around to face her. "I know, I know. But let's try not to bug each other either. We're both grown up, not just you. You've got to stop thinking of

14

me as your kid sister. We've got to live together as equals."

"But I am the oldest. I'm almost nineteen, and you're only fifteen and a half."

"Do you really think that makes such a difference?"

Becky sighed, then deliberately she bent over to kiss her sister's worried face. Stacey leaned over from the back and nuzzled against the two of them. The three girls held each other close.

When they released each other, Becky giggled. "That man must think we're crazy." She glanced toward a young man staring at them while putting bags of groceries into a jeep.

"Who cares?" Nancy tossed her head.

Becky, with Stacey clinging to her hand, followed Nancy into the market. She marveled, as she often did, that the three of them were sisters, since they looked so different. Other people said there was a strong family resemblance, but Becky couldn't see it. She considered Nancy the beauty of the family, with her creamy skin, her large, somber brown eyes and long, honey-colored hair. Nancy always looked trim and fresh, as if she had just stepped out of a cool, fragrant bath. Unlike Becky, her clothes matched and were spotless and unwrinkled.

While Nancy was softly rounded, Becky was narrow and lean in her body and face, her hair straight and black. She never felt as if her exterior matched her interior. Inside she felt soft and vulnerable, overwhelmed by the quick succession of emotions that seemed to constantly assault her; but when she looked at herself in a mirror, she was amazed that none of it showed. Her face looked strong, sometimes even stern, with its straight black eyebrows; narrow, slightly crooked nose; and full, firm mouth. Often she felt as if she were looking at a stranger.

Nine-year-old Stacey was the curly one. Sometimes Becky even called her Curly. Her blond hair was curly, her mouth curled up, and her soft little body often seemed to fold itself up into curls. She had been a smiling, happy child, but since the unhappy events of the past several months she had had nightmares and fits of temper and crying.

Nancy and Becky divided the shopping list between them, while Stacey ran between the two, unable to decide which one she wanted to stay with.

When they were back in the car with their groceries, Stacey immediately opened a bag of potato chips and began to eat.

"Let her do it," Becky advised Nancy, when she saw her sister's frown. "It's been a lousy, terrible day. Leave her alone."

"All right this time. But you and I have to have a talk. We have to make some plans, set up some rules."

Becky didn't answer, but she felt a familiar wave of impatience with Nancy's need for blueprints, for being in control. Becky had not wanted to think about what was going to happen next. For the past months—everything now dated from the accident—the present had absorbed all her emotions and energy. She felt as if there was no past and no future. There were times when she had lain in bed at night consciously trying to reconstruct a happy event, a time when her parents and the three sisters had been together laughing, playing a game, having a picnic. But she had never been able to fit in all the pieces. At some point her memory always would fail, she would get stuck on something silly like whether they had cooked hamburgers or Nancy had made one of her famous salads, and she would cry into her pillow. It didn't matter what they had eaten or what they had done, because now it was all wiped out—like taking an eraser and cleaning off a blackboard. Nothing was lasting, nothing was left. There was not even a reason for remembering, because no event mattered; each was temporary, and therefore meaningless.

After supper Becky took a basket and went in search of mushrooms. There was a stream behind their house that she crossed on a wooden footbridge. It led to a path up a long, tree-filled hill. She walked slowly, her eyes searching for the precious *Agaricus augustus* (her father had been precise about names) that came out in early spring. She had been right—the rain had brought them out. With a thrill of pleasure, Becky went up the hillside stooped over, picking. Her basket was almost full when she came to the crest where the woods opened up to meadows and from where, way below, she could see the Connecticut River. She loved this spot. There was one huge old oak that she and Nancy used to climb when they were younger. When you got up high enough you could see the whole valley and the river, almost as far as Long Island Sound. Becky sat down with her back against the tree and looked off into the valley.

She felt close to her father. Nancy had wanted to scatter his ashes here, but Becky had prevailed upon her not to. "I sit up there all the time," Becky had said, "and I couldn't bear it if his ashes were there. *He* is there, very close. I want to think of him alive, not dead."

Yet in her mind, most often when she was up in this

special place, Becky went over the events of the day he died. It had happened on a school day. Mr. Jones had been at work in a factory as usual, where his boss had sent him to repair a faulty pipe. The day had had a good start for Becky, for a social studies paper was returned marked A—. She was feeling euphoric when she got a message to go to the principal's office.

"I'm not worried," she had said to her friend Lisa. "I can't think of anything I've done." She walked through the halls gaily.

She was ushered into Mr. Prescott's office promptly, and as soon as she saw his face she knew something was wrong. "I'm afraid I've got some bad news for you," he had said, his usually cheerful face somber. "There's been an accident at the factory, and your father's been hurt."

Becky, who had been standing facing him, sat down. "Is it bad?"

"I'm afraid it's pretty serious. He's in the hospital. Your mother's there and she wants you to come. Mrs. Holmes will drive you over. I'm sorry, Becky. I hope everything will be all right."

"Thank you." In the outer office Mrs. Holmes, a teacher's aide, was waiting for her, and in a daze Becky went for her coat and then walked out to the parking lot. She was grateful that the older woman didn't talk much on the way. She was a good driver, and they got to the hospital quickly.

"Do you want me to go in with you?" Mrs. Holmes looked at her uncertainly.

"I don't think so, thank you. My mom's here. I'll be okay. Thanks for bringing me."

Mrs. Holmes reached over and took her hand. "Take care," she said simply.

Becky found Mrs. Jones and Nancy outside the emergency room. Her mother, a slim, frail woman at best, looked to Becky as if she had shrunk inches. Her face was white and pinched. Becky hugged them both. They told her that her father, an engineer working for a big contractor, had suffered severe third-degree burns over a good part of his body when a steam pipe he had been sent to examine had broken.

Becky's memory of the three of them sitting in a sort of open hallway, waiting for some news, was sharp. She remembered the hospital smell, and asking about Stacey. She was told that her mother had not wanted the little girl to come to the hospital, and Nancy had called a neighbor to pick her up at school. Nurses walked through the hallway. Some had serious faces and others went by laughing and talking. Becky had liked the laughing ones; they made her feel that her father was going to be okay.

The doctors were still discussing whether Mr. Jones could be moved to a burn center when, that night, he had died. Becky couldn't get over the fact that she hadn't been able to say good-bye to him. No one but her mother had been permitted to see him.

The next day Becky, her mother, and her two sisters had sat in their house, stunned. "I don't believe it, I just don't believe it," Stacey kept repeating. "He said yesterday morning he was going to play ball with me when he came home."

Neighbors and friends had come over bringing food, and men and women they had never met before had come from the place where their father had worked. Becky was glad to be kept busy, passing out the cakes and cookies, rinsing glasses, yet expecting any minute to see her father walk in the door with one of his sur-

19

prises. It could be Becky's favorite kind of salami that he had picked up at the Italian market, or some rare kind of fruit, or once a stray kitten he had seen on the road.

Stacey's repeated insistence that she didn't believe it got on Becky's nerves, but she felt the same way. People like her father didn't die. He had been too young, too full of life, the strong force in their family. He had been the one who had initiated the excursions, the games, the trips to the beach or the mountains. Their mother was the passive one. She had leaned on him heavily, seeking his advice in everything from choosing a new wallpaper pattern to asking what to wear to a party. He had always been so patient with her anxieties and fears, never scolding her for her fits of crying. "Your mother isn't feeling well," he would tell the girls when she went to her room and closed the door. "Let's not make too much noise."

But in her husband's death, Mrs. Jones was, for once, decisive. She didn't want a funeral. She had him cremated and didn't want the ashes. "He's already been burned," she had said bleakly, angrily. Becky had been frightened by the grim look on her mother's pinched face, afraid that if she reached out to touch her she might set off some dreadful violence of grief. She would have liked to have said, "Don't be in such a hurry. I don't believe he's dead."

There was no place to mourn, nowhere to go.

The only place Becky had was her tree, and she had spent hours up there. Their house had been impossible to stay in. Their father's sister, Aunt Marie, had come from Long Island, but Mrs. Jones had chased her out. "I want to be alone," she had said. "I don't want anyone fussing over me. Besides, she picks at her food. I can't stand to watch her eat."

But it was their mother who nervously watched everyone eat while she herself ate nothing. "She's like she was after Stacey was born," Nancy said, "only worse." Becky had always known her mother was frail and what people called "nervous." She remembered the crying after Stacey was born, but then she had been too young to understand.

After her father's death, Becky hated coming home from school. She was never sure what she would find, except she knew that the house would be a mess. Her mother had never been one of those women who took pride in spotless floors, but she had kept their modest house clean and neat. Since the accident, however, Mrs. Jones had withdrawn into a closed world of her own and seemed to care about nothing. The breakfast dishes would be in the sink, garbage could be on the floor as well as in the garbage pail, and her mother would be sitting in a rocker with the shades drawn. Nancy, who had graduated from high school, would still be at work. So Becky would send Stacey out to play and then begin cleaning up the house herself.

In the beginning Becky had tried to talk to her mother, to help her out of the painful prison she was living in; but she couldn't budge her. She and Nancy had tried to persuade her to go to a psychiatrist, but she had flatly refused. "What can a doctor do? Bring my husband and your father back?" she asked.

One day Becky had found her mother in the middle of the usual mess, but furiously removing the finish from one of the mahogany dining-room chairs they had. She had partly removed the stain from one chair

21

and then gone on to another. "She's going to ruin them all," Becky had said to Nancy, even though she thought they were rather ugly chairs anyway.

Nancy had shrugged. "It's better than just sitting, I suppose."

Then there had been the hideous day when Becky stood frozen in front of the kitchen door for seconds before she had drawn a deep breath and banged the door open. The smell of gas was horrible. All the windows were closed with towels stuffed around them, and her mother was on the floor in front of the open oven door. The gas was turned high without a fire to it.

Becky had yelled to Stacey, trailing behind her, to stay out. Instinctively she ran to her mother first and lifted her crumpled body so that she was sitting up. Then she ran around the room opening the windows, throwing the towels onto the floor. When she bent over her mother again, the fact that her mother was breathing made her tremble with relief. "Mom, Mom . . . " She had her arm around her, propping her up.

Her mother's eyes had fluttered, and then she sank down on the floor again. Becky stared at her for a few seconds and then flew to the telephone to call an ambulance. By this time Stacey had come in and was sitting on the floor beside her mother. "Mommy, Mommy . . . ," she was sobbing softly.

"She's going to be all right," Becky had assured her, wishing she was sure of it herself. When the two girls were riding to the hospital with their mother, Becky couldn't believe what was happening. Her own behavior had surprised her as much as anything. It was as if she had been in a play and someone else had been directing her movements. She felt empty of feelings.

"I don't know how you did it all," Nancy had said much later, when the sisters had left their mother in the hospital and were home. "I might have fainted and been useless."

"No, you wouldn't have. It was creepy, as if I'd done it all before and knew just what to do." Becky hadn't said it to her sister, but thinking about it in bed that night she was convinced that somehow her father had been the one directing her. She didn't believe in ghosts, yet she felt that his spirit had been with her during the whole ordeal of that day.

They had kept Mrs. Jones in the hospital several days for tests and put her in a psychiatric ward for a few weeks. When she came home the girls had tried to make it as easy and pleasant for her as possible, but their mother refused to be helped out of her withdrawal. She wouldn't watch television, she didn't want visitors, she wouldn't even leave the house to go marketing. She just sat and rocked. Nancy and Becky never left Stacey home alone with their mother for fear she might make another attempt at suicide. During the day, a few neighbors took turns coming in to check on her.

Sometimes Mrs. Jones would suddenly start to scream, or cry, or rip her clothes off. The girls were very frightened; and when the doctor said that their mother should be in a mental institution, they reluctantly agreed.

Becky had argued with Nancy. "Some of those places are awful," she said. "Why can't she just stay here. We can take care of her."

"We can't properly. She's alone most of the day and that's probably the worst thing for her. In a hospital they might be able to cure her."

"Once she's in there she'll never come out," Becky had said bleakly.

I lost that round, Becky thought that early evening as she sat under her tree watching the colors of the sky change with the spring sunset. She still felt she was right and that when they had left their mother at the Palmer Hospital in the afternoon they were closing a door that would never open. Thinking about it filled her with both an undefinable rage and a terrible sense of helplessness. She knew, if she let it, that her anger could direct itself toward Nancy, although she also knew it would be misplaced. Nancy was as trapped as she and as innocent too of responsibility for the awful things that had happened to their family. Yet in her older sister Becky felt a force that was threatening. For all Nancy's outward gentleness, her soft, domestic femininity, Becky recognized an iron will that would not bend, a bossiness that was determined to dominate.

Becky tried to shake these thoughts from her mind. This is bad thinking, she said to herself. All we have now is each other, and we're going to have to get along. I'm going to think of Nancy's good qualities, how pretty she is, the super-gooey desserts she makes, and remember that once she did let me wear her one and only cashmere sweater. Besides she's smart; she knows more about paints and wallpaper than her boss and she even partly decorated a house for a customer.

Yet the spark of rebellion persisted. To live with

24

Nancy without the placating affection of her parents, to have her sister telling her what to do, loomed ahead as a burden she did not relish.

Becky walked back down the hill slowly, carrying her basket of mushrooms. Some cars were parked in the driveway and Becky gave a deep sigh. She wished no one had come over. It should be just the three of us, she thought. For Becky it was a night of mourning.

2

Becky deposited her bag of mushrooms on the kitchen
table and headed for the stairs to go up to her room.
She quickly went by the open archway to the living
room where Nancy was talking with a neighbor, Mrs.
Marsh, and a man Becky recognized as Mr. Cannon,
who had come to see them after her father's accident.
Becky remembered that she had liked him because he
was a friend of her father's and had worked with him.
She hoped no one had seen her go by because she
didn't feel like being social.

Up in her room on the second floor of their old-fashioned house, she closed the door and flopped down on
her bed. Hers was a small room with a slanted ceiling
and dormer windows, but it was her sanctuary. At one
time she had shared a room with Stacey; this had been
a sewing-ironing-store room, until Becky had per-
suaded her parents to let her turn it into a bedroom.
She had made it very much her own, with huge posters
of jungle animals on the walls, two grotesque masks,
and an incongruous tall vase of bright artificial chrysanthemums standing in a corner. The furniture was

nondescript: an Indian print thrown over the studio bed, a white wicker porch chair next to the reading lamp, and a desk made of an old door held up by a battered metal file that Becky had painted a bright red.

Her body ached as if she had hiked twenty miles, and she had just kicked off her shoes and closed her eyes when she heard Nancy calling. "Becky, come on down."

Wearily Becky went to the head of the stairs. "I'm tired; can't I be excused, please?"

"This is important. I think you should be here." Nancy's voice was insistent.

Becky put on her shoes, ran a brush through her hair, and reluctantly went downstairs.

Mrs. Marsh, a round-faced plump woman who lived across the street from them, got up and put her arms around Becky. "You poor girls, what are you going to do, all by yourselves in this house? It's a shame, a terrible shame. You should have your aunt come live with you. I'd take care of you myself if I didn't have my own family."

Becky wriggled uncomfortably. "I think we'll be all right," she said, gently extricating herself from Mrs. Marsh's arms. "We'll manage." She looked across to catch Nancy's eye for her agreement, but Nancy looked as worried as Mrs. Marsh.

"I hope so," Nancy murmured. "It's a big responsibility taking care of two kids."

Becky bristled but kept her mouth shut, and went over to shake hands with Mr. Cannon.

After some more sorrowful head-shaking and murmurs of sympathy, Mrs. Marsh departed, to Becky's relief. Mr. Cannon seemed relieved too, and relaxed in his chair. "I've been telling your sister," he said to

Becky, "that you girls should see a lawyer. That factory had no business letting your father get near that pipe. The whole section should have been closed. It's a clear case of negligence on management's part, and you girls can collect a lot of money. I'll give you the name of a good, reliable firm if you want."

"But we already get workmen's compensation because of the accident," Becky said.

"Sure. You're entitled to that. This is separate. The workmen's compensation comes through the office where your father worked. But the factory was at fault. I think they were warned about the safety valve on the pipe before. Look, you've got nothing to lose by talking to a lawyer. He'll know if you've got a case."

"Sure, why not?" Becky said.

"I suppose so." Nancy looked dubious. "I hate getting mixed up with lawyers."

"If the factory was at fault, they should pay for it. Our father was *killed*." Becky's face was grim. "Money won't bring him back to life, but it can help Mom, and us. I'm all for it."

"I thought you would be," Nancy said a bit belligerently. She turned to Mr. Cannon with a weak smile. "Becky's the fighter in this family."

"That's all right, if you fight for the right things. Sometimes you have to fight." He gave Becky a smile that she returned gratefully.

Mr. Cannon wrote out the name and address of a law firm and handed it to Nancy. "If I can help in any way, let me know," he said, and with a warm pat on the shoulder for Becky, he left.

"I'm going to make some tea; want some?" Nancy asked.

28

"Yeah, I'll be down in a minute." Becky went upstairs and got out of her clothes and into a favorite long, hooded robe. Before going back down, she peeked into Stacey's room to find, as usual, that Stacey had kicked off her covers. Becky tucked them back around her baby sister and stared down at her for a minute or two. Stacey was the one both she and Nancy would have to take care of.

Nancy had the kettle boiling by the time Becky came downstairs. "I'm hungry," Becky announced. "I think I'll cook up my mushrooms." She turned to the kitchen table for her basket. "Where'd you put them?"

"I put them in the garbage. You weren't thinking of eating them, were you?" Nancy was filling two cups, each with a tea bag, with the hot water.

"You put them in the garbage? My beautiful mushrooms . . . of course I was going to eat them. What did you think I picked them for?" Becky was furious.

"How should I know? But you couldn't eat them, I wouldn't let you. All I need now is for you to kill yourself with some poisonous mushrooms. Honestly, Becky . . . "

"They were perfectly good. They're the same mushrooms that Dad always picked. I used to go with him, you know that. I *know* they were good." She lifted the lid to the garbage pail but quickly saw that the mushrooms, broken and mixed up with the rest of the spoiling food, were irretrievable. "I could murder you. It's a good thing Dad isn't here to see those mushrooms in the garbage pail. We always had such a good time getting them, they're special." She was almost in tears.

Nancy was concentrating on slicing a lemon, but she glanced up, and Becky was shocked to see how tight her face was. "Everything was special for you and Dad."

"What do you mean by that?" Becky asked tersely.

"Nothing, forget it." Nancy gave an unconvincing laugh. "Anyway, now we're even. Remember the time you threw away the piece of wedding cake I was going to sleep on? From Lucy's wedding. I could have killed you then. I was going to have some beautiful dream on it."

Becky looked at her sister in amazement. "You've been holding that against me all these years? I can't believe it. I was only eight years old then, younger than Stacey is now. And I didn't do it on purpose. I didn't even know there was any cake inside that dirty-looking white box. Yes, we're even," she added grimly. "I don't want any tea. Good night."

Back in her room, Becky got into her nightgown and under the covers. She wished she had taken the tea upstairs with her, to calm her down. She felt her stomach, always her weak spot, churning with anger. All the good thoughts she had had about Nancy earlier in the evening left her. She didn't know how they were going to manage. For a few minutes she even considered going to live with Aunt Marie, their only close relative. The thought made Becky giggle to herself softly. That would be the last, and worst, desperate move she could make. But she couldn't forget the look on her sister's face when she made her remark about Becky and their father.

A few days later, Becky got off the school bus at Lisa's house and went in with her for a soda. The girls lived a few blocks apart in Dorchester, locally known as a bedroom town. Their regional school, the shops, movie house, and restaurants were all in the neighboring town of New Salem. Their village consisted mainly of houses, a green with two churches, a library and one country store, and a small run-down neighborhood of old houses with a few stores near the railroad tracks.

"Becky, how are you and your sisters doing?" Mrs. Slovak, Lisa's mother, gave Becky a warm hug. "I worry about you."

"Thanks. I guess we're doing all right. Friday we're going to see a lawyer. A friend of my father's thinks we should sue the factory for negligence."

"I should think so. That accident was terrible." Mrs. Slovak had flashing, dark eyes and a pert, oval face that her daughter inherited. They were both short and slim, but Lisa had a dreamy look different from her mother's sharp alertness.

"We're going up to my room," Lisa announced, picking up a jar of peanut butter and some bread, and handing Becky two sodas.

"I know. You girls want to talk. Don't get crumbs all over the place."

Upstairs in Lisa's room, Lisa curled up on the bed while Becky sprawled on fat pillows scattered around the floor. "So, how are you doing?" Lisa asked. "Have you heard anything about your mother?"

"Nothing much. Nancy talks to the doctor, but he doesn't tell us anything except that she's getting along, whatever that means. You're lucky you've got your parents," she said forlornly.

"I know. Yet, in some ways, doesn't it feel good to be on your own? I don't mean that you don't miss your parents," she added hastily, "what happened is awful.

31

But until your mother is well and can come home, just the three of you there together could be pretty good too. There's no one to tell you what to do."

"That's what you think. There's my sister Nancy. She wants to tell me what to do all the time. It's all right for parents to tell you, but for a sister only three and a half years older to feel she has to be responsible for you . . . " Becky shook her head. "If we do get some money I'm going to leave home. That is, if Mom doesn't come back. I can take care of myself."

"How can you do that? They won't let you." Lisa spread a piece of bread with the peanut butter and handed it to Becky, then fixed one for herself.

"I don't know how I'm going to do it, but I'll find a way. And who's 'they'? Who can stop me?" Becky bit into her bread.

"I don't know—Nancy, people. A kid can't just pick up and leave home. The police pick up runaways."

"I wouldn't be a runaway. Who'd I be running away from if I have no parents at home? I don't see why I couldn't just live by myself someplace if I have the money." There was a note of desperation in Becky's voice. "I'll dig a cave. Will you come see me in my cave? Or maybe I'll live in the woods, and twenty years from now someone will find this wild woman eating berries and nuts and wearing a garland of leaves. The crazy kid with the crazy mother." She gave a short laugh, but her eyes were somber.

"Oh, Becky, your mother will come home; everything will be all right." Lisa looked at her with sad eyes.

"Sure. Everything will be fine." Becky managed a weak grin.

3

Friday afternoon Nancy and Stacey were waiting for Becky when she came out of school. "You could have worn a skirt," Nancy said, eyeing Becky's crumpled jeans.

"Why? We're going to see if we want to hire him, aren't we? We don't have to impress *him*, do we? Or her. There are lady lawyers, aren't there?"

"Sure, but this one happens to be a man."

"I hope he's nice," Stacey said. "What do lawyers do exactly?"

"They present cases before a judge and often a jury. They know about the law and try to prove their client is right," Becky told her.

"That's simplifying it," Nancy laughed. She parked in front of an old building on a side street. She had taken trouble with her appearance and looked pretty in a tweed skirt and dark-red cardigan. Inside, the girls found that they had to walk up a long flight of stairs to reach the lawyer's office on the second floor. "He must be poor," Stacey remarked, "having his office in a place like this."

"Mr. Cannon said it was a top firm," Nancy said. "Maybe they prefer it this way."

Becky liked the old-fashioned office with its dark wood paneling and worn leather chairs; she felt confidence in a firm that didn't feel the need to jazz up their place with modern fixtures and chrome. She liked it even more when a gray-haired secretary ushered them into the spacious office of Leonard Timmins, the head of the firm. He had been seated behind a tremendous oak desk, but he stood up courteously to greet them. He was what Becky's mother would have called "a gentleman of the old school." He was in his sixties, dressed in a conservative three-piece suit with a watch chain draped across his generous bulk. His eyes squinted under his bushy eyebrows, but his look was sharp; his prominent nose and jutting chin indicated a strong mind behind his long, homely face.

He arranged chairs facing his desk for the three girls and sat back down in his own swivel chair. "Now, tell me what it is that you young ladies have on your mind." He looked from one to the other, but it was Nancy who answered him. She told him the story of their father's accident and his death, and their mother's ensuing illness. She ended by saying that Mr. Cannon, who had recommended this firm, thought they should sue the factory.

"Mmm . . . it sounds as if you have a reasonable and justified lawsuit; but of course I can't say anything definite until I make some inquiries and we do our homework." He asked Nancy a few more specific questions about their father's work, how long he had been with his firm, and what his background and experience had been. He kept nodding his head as Nancy spoke, and Becky found this encouraging.

When it seemed the interview was coming to an end, Becky said, "May I ask a question?"

"Certainly. What would you like to know?" Mr. Timmins asked.

"If we do get money, would it be evenly divided among the three of us? Would we each get a lump sum?"

Mr. Timmins looked a bit startled, but he took her question seriously and his manner was thoughtful when he answered. "That will depend on how well your mother is. If she is able to manage, I believe the award would be given to her. The suit may be made in her name, on her behalf; we will have to see about that when the time comes. If she is incapacitated, then we would probably sue on behalf of you three girls and your mother. Then it would be determined how the money be handled, whether it should be put in trust or what. That will also depend on how much money there is," he added with a smile. "All that has to come later."

"Yes, of course. I was just wondering."

"Feel free to ask any questions you want," Mr. Timmins said. "Now I want to introduce you to my young associate, David Cimino. I will turn over all this to him, and he will handle the details. Of course we will discuss it together." He clipped together the papers on which he had been making notes and pressed a buzzer for his secretary. When she put her head in the doorway, he asked her to send in Mr. Cimino.

Mr. Cimino, considerably younger than Mr. Timmins, was a dark, bearded man with a brooding face.

Not handsome, Becky thought, but interesting. He also was dressed conservatively, but he had an intense air and challenging look in his eyes that made you suspect he was not as conventional as he appeared.

He lived up to her expectations when, after the introductions were made, he looked at Nancy and said, "I hope you are not here to ask us to defend you for some heinous crime."

"I don't think so," Nancy said, startled.

Mr. Cimino grinned. "Good. But you have that sweet, innocent look reminiscent of a client I once had who stabbed her ex-lover. Remember Miss Casey?" he asked as he turned to Mr. Timmins.

"How could I forget her? But I can assure you these young ladies have committed no crime. They have an interesting case; I will go over it with you." After some small conversation, Mr. Cimino led them out of the office.

"That young guy was weird," Nancy said when they were down the stairs and getting into the car. "I hope he's a good lawyer."

"He didn't take his eyes off you," Becky said. "I think it was love at first sight. He wanted to say something crazy to impress you."

Nancy gave her a sidelong glance. She was sometimes surprised by her sister's perception, since she too had been aware of Mr. Cimino's eyes on her. But she shook her head negatively. "Don't be silly. He was simply showing off. I wonder if he got that woman off. . . . But you certainly seemed awfully worried about the money. I thought that was a strange question."

"Why? If we're going to get the money, I think it

should be divided evenly. That is if Mom isn't home...."

"But Mom will be home, won't she?" Stacey asked.

The two older girls exchanged glances. "We hope so," Becky said.

Becky had been thinking a great deal about money since their mother had gone to the mental hospital. One evening Nancy had insisted that the three of them sit down to discuss their finances. "We have to work out a budget," she said.

"You work it out, you know more about it than we do," Becky had suggested. "You handle money in the store all the time, and you're the only one earning any real money. It's not that complicated, is it? You write down everything we spend, and then we can divide up what's left over, or you keep it."

"I'm not sure there's going to be anything left over. We barely have enough to cover what we need. I'm trying not to dip into the little savings account or use up Dad's insurance money. It wasn't much to start with. We'd be left with only the workmen's compensation."

"I don't need a baby-sitter, I don't mind staying here alone when you two go out," Stacey offered, "if I can stay up and watch TV and you don't come home too late."

"We'll have to see about that," Nancy said, sounding like their mother.

"I'll take my lunch to school—it'll be cheaper. The lunches they serve aren't so good anyway," Becky said.

The discussion ended up with Nancy doing a lot of figuring and saying that they should try to cut down on using gas for the car, and that they'd eat more spaghetti and less meat. "And I know I shouldn't fill up the kettle when I want to make one cup of tea," Becky said to Nancy, who was often pointing that out to her. "And use the tea bag a second time."

Nancy laughed. "Don't go overboard."

It didn't take Becky long to figure out that having money was a very important part of being independent and free. After the visit to the lawyer's office she thought all the more about it, and the possibility of being on her own. The news about their mother wasn't good. It was about a week after they had seen the lawyers that Nancy said she had spoken to the doctor. It was Saturday morning, and the girls had walked to the village library and were on their way home. "Mom isn't doing well," Nancy said after Stacey had left them to go to a friend's house. "I spoke to the doctor yesterday."

"You waited a long time to tell me," Becky commented.

"I didn't have a chance. I didn't want to talk in front of Stacey, she gets so upset. Anyway, he said she didn't respond to the shock treatments, so they had to be stopped. He didn't say much except that there's no improvement. I have a feeling she may be worse," Nancy added dismally.

"I wish we could go to see her. I hate not seeing how she is ourselves. It's so hard to know what to think or believe."

"We have to trust the doctors, that's all we can do."

Becky frowned. "If Dad was here he'd find out. He wouldn't just leave it to the doctors."

"Well, Dad isn't here." Nancy's voice was harsh.

38

"Sometimes I think you're glad he's not," Becky shot back.

"That's a stupid thing to say." They had stopped walking, and Nancy leaned back against a white fence. "But I didn't worship him the way you did. You were always his favorite anyway." Nancy's face was so tense Becky didn't answer. Wow, she thought, she was jealous of Dad and me! It was a startling revelation that was going to demand a lot of thinking through.

Becky started to walk on, and Nancy came alongside her.

They stopped to talk to Mrs. Marsh, who was out walking her dog. "Mom's getting along fine," Becky said in answer to her inquiry.

"What did you say that for?" Nancy asked when they were past her.

"I guess because I can't bear to think that she isn't. Besides, it's no one's business how Mom is," Becky said morosely. "I don't want to believe that she's never really coming home, and yet I do believe it. Look, the dogwood's out. I hate it being spring—usually spring is such a happy time."

"I have some other news." Nancy spoke in her normal voice. "That Mr. Cimino from the law office called me. He asked me to meet him for lunch next week. He has some papers for Mom to sign that give me power of attorney. He says that should be done regardless of the case so that I can legally handle everything." Nancy pulled a few leaves from the hedge that they passed. "It only means I can draw money from the bank and sign checks, things like that," she added, seeing Becky's face harden.

"Yes, I know," Becky said, but she thought this was another tightening of Nancy's dominance over herself and Stacey. She didn't like it.

"I told you Mr. Chimino fell for you. He could have asked you to just pick up the papers at the office." Becky was amused by her sister's blush.

"He was very nice on the phone. But I'm worried about bothering Mom to sign papers. It may upset her."

"Why don't you just send them to the doctor and ask him to do it," Becky suggested.

Nancy gave her an admiring glance. "Sometimes you can be so sensible," Nancy said.

"And other times so cuckoo," Becky said, still keeping her voice light. "That's part of my charm."

When they got home Becky announced that she was going out to pick more mushrooms. "And you won't have a chance to throw them away," she told Nancy. "I'm going to take them to the store to sell them."

"You are cuckoo. No one is going to buy wild mushrooms that you picked. They'd be afraid."

"Just because you don't trust me doesn't mean no one else does. Sometimes, Nancy, you give me a pain."

Becky said this good-naturedly, but Nancy answered coldly, "The feeling is mutual."

Suddenly the two girls were glaring at each other. Becky gave a deep sigh. She felt their recent, quick anger with each other had deep roots she had never known about. "You like to tell me off, but if I say one word of criticism about you, you freeze. You can dish it out, but you can't take it. What are you going to do today?" Purposely she changed the subject.

"I'm going to shop with a customer for a rug. She's doing over her upstairs and I'm helping her." They were in their kitchen and Nancy dumped an envelope of wallpaper samples onto the table. "These are for her bedroom and bathroom. I hope she picks the ones I like."

"Is she nice? Rich?" Becky was wiping out her basket for the mushrooms.

"Nice and pretty rich. But she has a husband who looks like a fish." Nancy spread the paper samples out so she could look at them.

"Is that why you picked paper with mermaids and seashells?"

"Oh, my, I never thought of that. But I don't think he knows he looks like a fish," Nancy said quite seriously.

"His wife might," Becky said.

Nancy laughed. "I won't be able to keep a straight face when I show these to her."

The girls laughed together. "I could really get along with you if I didn't have to live with you," Becky remarked, only half joking.

4

With her basket of mushrooms on her arm, Becky walked the half-mile or so to the village store. Mr. Schultz, the store owner, was a ruddy-faced man who called everyone in town by their first name and carefully avoided taking sides in any town controversy. "Good morning, Becky," he said jovially. "How are you?"

"I'm okay." Then, to Becky's dismay, she saw his face change to a sober expression; he's remembered "our tragedy," Becky thought. "And your mother?" he asked.

"She's doing all right," Becky told him. "I just picked these mushrooms," she went on hurriedly. "Do you think you could sell them?"

Mr. Schultz peered into Becky's basket and shook his head. "I'm sorry, I couldn't possibly sell wild mushrooms. Everyone would be afraid. You'd better not eat them yourself."

"They're perfectly good. Delicious, believe me. My father used to pick them all the time."

Mr. Schultz looked at the brown-and-orange mushrooms dubiously. "They look poisonous to me. Don't take any chances, Becky. Good mushrooms often have a poisonous twin. Only an expert can tell the difference."

"You don't trust me?"

He laughed. "Not when it comes to mushrooms." He turned away to wait on a customer. Becky was about to leave the store when she heard her name called. She turned around to face a tall boy with thick, fair hair and deeply set brown eyes. "I'll buy your mushrooms. How much are they?"

She looked at the boy in astonishment. She had heard that Mr. Schultz had hired a good-looking new assistant. Word gets around fast in a small town.

He smiled apologetically. "I heard Mr. Schultz call you Becky. You didn't see me, but I've seen you in here before. I'm Tim Harmon. I'm working for Mr. Schultz. I'm new in town. My dad works for the brass factory and he just got transferred here."

Becky looked the boy up and down. He *was* attractive, with a sun-tanned skin, an expensive haircut, and a tense, aristocratic face. "Your father's one of the executives over there?"

"I guess you'd call him that. Middle, not top. He's not a big shot, if that's what you mean. What's the matter?"

"Nothing. Aren't you afraid of these mushrooms?"

"You said they were okay, didn't you?"

"Sure they're okay." She looked at him curiously. "But you don't know me. I could be careless. . . ." She gave him a sly glance. "I could go around murdering people. Who knows?"

43

Tim laughed. "You don't look like a murderer. I'll tell you what, I only work half-day today. I could cook them for lunch and we'll both eat them. That way I'll know they're safe."

"You know how to cook?"

"I'm a terrific cook. I could make you a mushroom omelet like you never tasted before." He looked at her questioningly.

Becky hesitated. She was in the mood for an adventure. And he trusted her, not like her sister Nancy. "Come over to my house," she said impulsively. "You can cook there." She wondered if he'd say yes.

"Sure, where do you live?"

"Near where the mushrooms grow." She gave him a quick smile, and then directions. "What time?"

"Around one."

"Okay."

On the way home, Becky felt excited. Then she realized that she hadn't gotten any money for her pickings, and wouldn't get any. I should have sold them to that boy, she thought ruefully. But wait till she told Lisa she had invited the new boy to her house for lunch.

Once home, Becky rushed around straightening up the downstairs rooms, picking up Stacey's crayons, old magazines, and sneakers from the floor, and giving a quick dusting to the furniture. Then she tackled the kitchen and washed the pots and dishes accumulated from the day before.

By the time Tim arrived she had washed her face and put on a clean shirt. He came bringing a bag of fresh rolls from the store, and he too had changed his shirt. With the sleeves of his crisp blue oxford rolled up to the elbows he looked efficient and ready to get to work. Tim gave a quick glance around the kitchen. "Hope you've got herbs and spices. That's how I like to cook."

"I suppose we have. I'm not big on cooking. My sister does most of it."

"You're not the domestic type, are you?" He was poking around the kitchen shelves looking to see what was there. He gave a shout of delight when he discovered a good variety of herbs and spices on a shelf. "Hooray. We're in business. Where are the eggs? And how many are we feeding?"

"I guess just you and me. My sisters aren't home. How many eggs do you want?"

Tim had carefully selected a bowl from a nest of them on a shelf and put it on the counter. "What about your parents? Aren't they home?"

Becky looked up at him abruptly. "No. My father's dead and my mother's in a mental hospital." She said it flatly, and made it clear she didn't want to discuss it further.

"I'm sorry." Tim looked at her and got the message, but his eyes told her that he truly was sorry. "Do you think four eggs will be enough for the two of us, or should I do more?"

"I'll tell you about it sometime," Becky said, apologizing for her abruptness.

"That's okay. I can understand your not wanting to talk about it."

Tim made the omelet with the mushrooms he had sautéed, and the two of them sat down to eat. "Well, here goes," Tim said, taking his first bite of the mushrooms. "If I start writhing on the floor, put me out of my agony so I have a quick death."

"I wouldn't know how," Becky said, "except to give you more mushrooms."

"You could choke me," he suggested.

"With my bare hands? Me, who won't even step on a spider? Besides," she said, taking a large mouthful of the egg and mushrooms, "so far you look pretty healthy. I'm afraid you're going to live."

"I'll tell you a secret," Tim said with a wide grin. "I really know all about mushrooms, so I knew these were okay."

Becky laughed with him. "And I thought you were so trusting. I'm the innocent. Do you like living here?"

"I haven't had much chance to find out. We've only been here a short while. It seems okay. I'll be going away to school in the fall, anyway."

"Where are you going?"

He gave her a shy glance. "Don't laugh. I want to be a cook, a chef really. I'm hoping to go to the Culinary Institute. It's a terrific place."

"I wouldn't laugh. My father loved to cook. There's nothing wrong with a man cooking. If a woman can be a truck driver, a man can be a cook."

"You and your sisters, you live here all alone?" Tim got up and filled the kettle with water for coffee. Becky marveled at how at home he had made himself in their kitchen.

"Yeah, all alone."

"That must be kind of fun."

"That's what all my friends think; but it's not that great. We had more fun when my parents were here. My older sister bugs me. If we're going to be alone, I'd rather really be alone, be by myself; that would really be neat."

Tim looked at her admiringly. "You mean have your own pad, come and go as you please? Boy, wouldn't I love that."

"Oh, well, it won't happen for me. My mother will come home and we'll almost be a family again." She smiled cheerfully at Tim, but there was a note of sadness in her voice.

Tim was gone before Stacey came home, soon followed by Nancy. "You had company," Stacey announced to Becky.

"How do you know?" Becky asked, somewhat annoyed.

"Mrs. Marsh told me. I met her outside, and she said my sister was entertaining a young man. Who was it?" Stacey bit into one of the rolls Tim had left.

"Someone you don't know," Becky said crossly. "Does that Mrs. Marsh watch everything we do?"

"She called us 'poor orphans,' but I told her we weren't poor and we had a mother so aren't orphans," Stacey said complacently. "That shut her up."

"Good for you," Becky said, and they both laughed.

Nancy came in then and wanted to know what the joke was. Stacey repeated the conversation. "Becky had a boyfriend here," she ended up saying.

"Who?" Nancy asked.

Becky told her about Tim and the mushrooms. "I guess the mushrooms didn't kill you," Stacey remarked. "I'm glad."

Nancy was frowning. "But you didn't know anything about this boy. Bringing him back here to the house when you were alone . . . I don't like it. That was a silly thing to do."

"He's working for Mr. Schultz, and his father works for the brass factory. It isn't as though I picked him up on the street. The kids in school all know who he is. We're not living in a big city! Besides, Mr. Schultz wouldn't hire just anyone," Becky protested.

"How do you know? Remember that baby-sitter who was raped by someone everyone thought was a nice boy, but it turned out no one actually knew a thing about him? Too many terrible things are happening today. Don't ever do anything like that again."

"I think I can take care of myself," Becky said, trying hard to keep her cool. "Of course anything can happen, we know all about that. No one expected Daddy's accident. But I'm not going around being scared all the time. It's a stupid way to live."

"While you are living here with me and I'm responsible for you, you'll just have to stick to the rules." Nancy's mouth was tight.

"No one made you responsible for me," Becky yelled. "And you have no right to make up rules. Stacey and I have as much right as you have."

"She's right," Stacey said. "We should vote on everything. This is a free country."

"I'm responsible because I'm the oldest. Both of you are minors, remember that," Nancy said with some dignity.

"I don't want to be a miner," Stacey said. "I won't go into any tunnels."

"Not that kind of a miner," Becky said, "it's kids who are underage. But just being older," she added, turning to Nancy, "doesn't make you smarter or give you the right to boss us. You're making everything impossible. We could get along fine if you understood that the three of us are all equals. We don't need a boss."

"I am *not* a boss, but you do do dumb things." Nancy intimated an end to the discussion; but Becky was furious.

"I'd like to know what. Dad really taught me about mushrooms, and I know about them; there was no mistaking these. Tim was a perfect gentleman the whole time he was here. As it happens he is a very nice guy. Besides, there's no place to go in this town. You should be glad I bring my friends home. When I do something dumb I'm willing to admit it, but I think my judgment is as good as yours." With that she walked out of the kitchen and went up to her room.

She hated these flare-ups with Nancy. When they were over, she was left not so much with anger as with an enveloping loneliness. Nancy's notions of sisters was so different from hers—Nancy only thought of being responsible, while Becky had a fantasy of intimacy, of exchanging confidences, of a cozy relationship filled with love and support.

She had read a book once when she was around ten about sisters, The Corner House Girls, and the image had stayed with her of an idyllic existence of girls living together and having fun together. It was a constant shock to her that Nancy and she couldn't be that way. She remembered Nancy's face when she had talked about Becky and their father: a pent-up rage against their closeness. As if it was my fault, Becky thought, or was something meant to hurt her.

It was Saturday night, and Becky felt like doing something. She called Lisa, but her friend had a date. There was no one else she felt like calling so late. She thought of Tim, but she didn't feel she knew him well enough to call him. Besides, he was probably out.

Restlessly she went back downstairs. "Want to play Monopoly?" she asked Nancy.

"Not really. I brought home a book this morning I want to read. Why don't you read one of your books?"

"I don't feel like reading." Becky wandered from one room to another. Stacey was watching television.

After about ten or fifteen minutes Nancy put down her book. "What's the matter with you? You're as jumpy as a cat. I wish you'd settle down to something."

"There's nothing I feel like settling down to. I guess I'll go for a walk." Becky picked up a sweater she had left in the kitchen.

"Alone, at night? I don't think that's a good idea," Nancy said.

"Nothing's going to happen to me," Becky said. "I'm not going far."

She went out quickly before Nancy could say anything more. It was a mild, misty evening, and Becky walked down the street slowly. She could see inside the brightly lit houses on both sides of the street, and it seemed to Becky that the families living in them had to be all happy and loving and enjoying themselves. Of course she knew they weren't; Mrs. Marsh was always quarreling with her husband, the Stoddards had a nagging old aunt living with them, the Cohens had a little girl in the hospital. Yet the houses and the lights looked so cozy and secure she didn't want to think that the families weren't the same way.

When she returned home Becky announced that she was going to make brownies. As she, Nancy, and Stacey sat in the kitchen and ate brownies and drank milk before going to bed, Becky felt she had accomplished something.

"We should do this every night," Stacey remarked.

"I'd get too fat," Nancy said between mouthfuls.

"I guess it wouldn't be special if we did it every night," Stacey mused.

"No, it wouldn't be," Becky said thoughtfully. "You're right, there have to be everyday things and special things."

"Yeah," Stacey agreed, "except I like special things every day."

Becky and Nancy laughed. "Me too," Becky said.

5

"You're all dressed up. Where are you going?" Stacey asked Nancy the following Wednesday morning when she appeared at breakfast in a blue corduroy suit and a new pink blouse.

"I've got a date for lunch," Nancy told her.

"With that lawyer," Becky added.

"Is he your boyfriend?" Stacey asked.

"Of course not. I hardly know him. This is business, for all of us."

"I hope he makes us rich," Stacey said. "If he does, I want a bike. And new sneakers."

"I think you need the sneakers even if we're not rich," Becky said, glancing at Stacey's worn ones.

All day at school Becky's mind kept wandering to what was happening at Nancy's lunch. Surely Mr. Cimino would know by now if they had a case and should sue. Becky daydreamed about how it would feel to be rich. Maybe they'd move into a big house when their mother came home. She imagined one of the elegant old houses in the village with a swimming pool and gardens, a servant for their mother, and a car of her own when she turned sixteen. Or maybe she would go away to boarding school in Boston, get away from Nancy and the dull life in Dorchester. She had visited Boston a few times with her father when he had gone there on business. She had loved walking around the streets, pretending she was grown up and living there by herself, going down to the market near the waterfront and to all the shops in Faneuil Hall.

After school, instead of taking the bus home, she decided to go over to the store where Nancy worked. It was a sunny mild day and Becky enjoyed the walk from school to New Salem's Main Street where the shops were. The paint and wallpaper store was in a recently renovated old building. It was set back discreetly from the street behind a red-brick walk lined on both sides with pots of greenery.

Nancy was busy with a customer but she greeted Becky and motioned her to sit down. Becky watched her sister admiringly. Nancy was cool and efficient, and looked as if she belonged. Becky wondered, as she often did, how they could have come from the same parents. Unlike herself, Nancy seemed to know exactly where she was going, from one point in life to another, without floundering. Becky felt a twinge of envy; and yet she did not want to be like Nancy. For all the emotional turmoil she always seemed to be enduring, and in spite of her lack of stylishness and ability to ever have her clothes match, she cherished her emotions. Secretly she was glad that she yelled and wept and laughed and went from one extreme to another while Nancy kept an even cool. At least, she thought ruefully, she was glad most of the time—except when she was annoyed with herself for taking everything so hard.

"So tell me, tell me, what did Mr. Cimino have to say?" Becky asked when Nancy's customer had left with a batch of wallpaper samples under her arm.

"Don't get excited, there's nothing much to tell. I have the papers for Mom to sign, and he agreed it was a good idea to send them to the doctor. And he thinks we have a case. He's optimistic, but you know lawyers; he won't say that he's sure we can win. But he thinks there is evidence of negligence. We'll have to prove it. He hopes we can settle out of court—it would be much cheaper and faster."

"Nancy, won't it be wonderful if we get rich?" Then Becky's face darkened with anger. "As if money could make up for Dad, or Mom's being sick. I almost don't want it. I may hate the money if we get it."

"That would be pretty silly. I feel just the opposite—they should pay for all they're worth. They shouldn't get away scot-free."

Becky sighed. "I know. Except if I buy something I want terribly with that money, it will always seem such an awful way to have gotten it. I may not enjoy it."

"It will just be money. I've got to get to work; you'd better go on home. How will you get there?"

"I'll bum a ride," Becky said.

Nancy looked stern. "You know you shouldn't be hitching rides."

"Oh, Nancy! Anyone going to the village is bound to be someone I know. Don't worry."

"Famous last words. How can I not worry? You can do foolish things."

54

"You keep saying that, but what have I done? You have some image in your head of me you won't get rid of. Either that or you like to worry."

Nancy gestured her to be on her way. "Go on home. Coming here instead of taking your bus was silly. You could have waited until tonight."

"Nuts." Becky waved a good-bye and walked out of the store.

Becky felt pretty smug when she quickly got a ride home with their plumber. She wished Nancy could see her sitting up front in his pickup truck. He dropped her off in front of the village store, and hesitantly she went inside to look for Tim. She had been disappointed that she hadn't heard from him since their lunch together; but she felt brave today.

She found him in the back of the store putting away crates of fruits and vegetables unloaded from a truck. His face lit up when he saw her. "Hi, I've been thinking about you. Picking more mushrooms?"

"No, they're finished. I thought maybe mine had killed you. I haven't seen you around."

"I don't notice you looking very sad about it," he laughed. "I was away. I had to go down to the Institute for an interview, and then I went to New York to see my grandmother. I was going to send you a card but I couldn't find a stamp."

"Yeah, I'm sure. New York was fresh out." Becky stood watching him.

"Did you ever try to find a post office in New York? They hide them away in dark alleys, honest. Anyway, I'm glad you came by. Have an apple?" He picked a ripe red one for her.

"Thanks." She sat on an upturned crate munching

her piece of fruit, enjoying the bright sun and the fresh smell of the produce. "It's nice to watch you work."

"I'll be through with this soon. What are you doing tonight? There's an old Woody Allen movie playing. Want to go see it?"

"If I can afford it."

"I'm inviting you."

Becky sat up with a bright face. "That's nice. Sure, I'd love it. I love Woody Allen."

"Good. I'll pick you up in time for the seven o'clock, okay?"

"Fine. See you then."

Becky walked home feeling very good.

When Stacey came home she found Becky furiously cleaning the house. The vacuum cleaner was out, and she was mopping the kitchen floor. "What's got into you?" Stacey asked. "You must have a fever."

"Oh, I have. I'm dying of a mysterious disease." Becky put her hand dramatically to her head. "But I'll die in a clean house, and you can bury me with my beloved mop and detergent."

"You're crazy," Stacey said complacently.

"Of course I am." Becky grinned at her. She went into a dance with the mop. "Do you believe in love at first sight?"

Stacey looked at her suspiciously. "No. Tom Hansen wrote me a note and said he loved me the minute he saw me. But he wears such thick glasses he couldn't see me if he fell over me. I don't believe you can love anyone at first sight. I couldn't."

"Oh dear, how did I ever have two such sensible sisters? You're so unromantic."

Becky was still feeling charged when Nancy came

home. Nancy however was not enthusiastic about her going out with Tim Harmon. "I forgot about that guy," Nancy said. "I still don't know anything about him. Or his family."

"You'll have a chance to meet him tonight. He's picking me up. You can give him your stamp of approval. He's good looking," Becky said amiably.

"Leave it to you to pick someone new in town. David calls you an original. He considers that a compliment." Nancy looked uncertain.

"I do too. You can thank him for me. I see it's David now, not Mr. Cimino," she added with a grin.

"Everyone calls people by their first names these days," Nancy said.

"Sounds pretty cozy to me," Becky said with something resembling a snort.

"Don't be ridiculous. I am not "cozy" with David Cimino."

"I wish you two would shut up," Stacey said, coming in from watching her television show. "I can hardly hear. Besides," she said, curiosity eating her up, "I'd like to know what you're fighting about."

"We're not fighting," Becky said with some dignity. "We're having an ordinary conversation."

"It doesn't sound that way to me," Stacey said. She looked from one to the other and laughed. "I don't know what you two would do without me to keep peace around here." She spoke in a grown-up, put-upon way that made both Becky and Nancy laugh.

That was the end of their conversation, but Becky felt she had not heard the last of Nancy's bugging her about Tim. She was determined, however, not to let what she considered Nancy's unjustified concern about who he was affect her.

She was up in her room getting dressed for the evening when Stacey came in. "I hate it when you and Nancy fight," Stacey said.

"Don't take it seriously. We weren't really fighting. I just don't want her to run my life. She thinks she has to take care of me, but I don't need anyone to do that. You're still a little kid and you do, but she thinks of us both the same way. I have to think things out for myself and make my own decisions. I have to grow up and be responsible for myself, you see?"

"I don't want you to grow up." Stacey put her arms around Becky. "I want you to stay the way you are."

Becky hugged her. "People don't stay the same. You're going to change, everyone does."

"I wish they didn't," Stacey moaned. "I wish nothing had changed."

"I know, I know." Becky held her until she stopped her quiet moaning.

Becky dressed carefully for her date with Tim, not in her usual quick, helter-skelter fashion, She chose a thin, India-print skirt and a plum-colored blouse that set off her dark eyes and hair. She went so far as to put on a touch of eye shadow and earrings. Stacey told her she looked beautiful when she came downstairs, and Nancy remarked drily, "I wish you bothered that much all the time."

"Then you'd tell me I was vain," Becky said teasingly.

"That is one thing I wouldn't accuse you of. You have a pretty healthy ego, but that's a different matter. But you do look nice."

"Thanks. Your own ego's not so bad," Becky retorted.

"Have I got an ego? Whatever that is, I want one too." Stacey looked inquiringly at her sisters.

"Yeah, you've got one, don't worry. I've got to go now." Tim was at the door and Becky asked him to come in to meet her sisters. He shook hands cordially with both. After a few minutes of conversation, he said that he and Becky had better leave or they'd be late for the movie.

"Have a good time," Nancy said.

Once in the car, Becky let out a sigh of relief. "My sister wanted to meet you and now thank goodness she has. Maybe she won't chew me out anymore for going out with you. She probably won't tell me what she thinks, though. Not like me. With me, it all hangs out. I guess that's why I get into trouble. If I don't like someone, it shows."

"That's more honest," Tim said. "What does she want to know about me? I've been to five different schools in the last ten years. I got A's in English and math and I flunked French. My parents go to the Congregational Church sometimes, my father is a trouble-shooter and my mother won a cup in golf. I had all the childhood diseases and I once broke my leg." He grinned at her. "Now you know."

"I think Nancy wanted to know how many girls you raped."

"Oh, dozens, all the time. What's with your sister, anyway? She got sex on the brain?"

Becky laughed. "Personally I think she's scared stiff of it. But why did you move so much? She'd be suspicious of that."

"My father's job. It's lousy. I hope we stay here." He gave her a sidelong glance. "This place has some interesting attractions."

59

"So the Chamber of Commerce says," Becky said with a sly grin. "A respectable quiet community . . . "

"That is not what I was thinking of," Tim said.

In the movie she liked the way Tim casually picked up her hand and held it. It was direct and warm, nicer than the way other boys had mumbled silly things to her, thinking that if they told her she was terrific she'd let them kiss her.

When they came out of the theater, Tim suggested that they go for pizza or a hamburger. "That would be nice," Becky agreed.

But once in the car, Becky said, "I've got an idea. Let's get a pizza and eat it down by the river."

"Now? At night?"

"Sure, why not? You scared?"

"No, I'm not scared. Just surprised. I don't even know where to get down to the water."

"I do. I know a path, and there are wonderful rocks to sit on when you get there. It'll be gorgeous tonight." She peered out of the car at the almost full moon. "It'll be exciting."

"You like excitement?" Tim asked, pulling the car into the pizza place.

"I love it. The good kind, not the bad. Not accidents."

With the hot pizza resting on the back seat of the car, Tim followed Becky's direction to a road that ran alongside the river and parked in a small clearing. Giving Becky a flashlight from the glove compartment, he told her to take the lead while he followed with the pizza box. She led him on a steep path down to the river. As she had said, it ended in a group of large rocks that jutted out into the water. Becky scampered out as far as she could, but Tim, carrying the pizza, followed more slowly. "Say, be careful," he called out. "You'll land in the water."

"Maybe I'll jump in," Becky called back. She stood poised at the edge of the farthest-out rock, facing the water as if to dive in. She had laid the flashlight down, and held her arms outstretched in front of her in a diving position.

"Becky!" Tim called out sharply.

She turned around laughing. "I was just fooling."

"Don't fool that way; you could give me a heart attack."

Tim joined her on the big rock, put the pizza carefully on a flat area, and pulled her down beside him. "Stay here, where I can hold onto you. I don't trust you."

"You're wise. I'm not reliable."

"Funny, I thought you were the good, solid, steady sort. After all, I did eat your wild mushrooms. Tell me more about yourself." He reached over and opened the pizza box, handed her a slice, and took one for himself.

Becky munched on her pizza for a few minutes before replying. Then she said, "I wish I knew what I am," she said musingly. "I feel so—I don't know, displaced. Everything's changed so fast and for no reason. If I had jumped off that rock and drowned, what difference would it make? A person can die or get killed at any time. You wouldn't know. You haven't had any tragedy happen in your life, have you?"

Tim finished his slice and took another before speaking. "Not like you have. But I can't say everything is glorious. I mean, moving around so much. Of course it's nothing like your father getting killed, but there are other things." Becky waited for him to elaborate, and after a few minutes he continued. "It's a good thing my parents just had me. They're okay, but they never should have had any family. We never do things together the way other people do. My father goes off on fishing trips in between jobs, but he never takes me. He goes with his friends. He took me once, and it was a disaster." Tim took his third slice of pizza and handed Becky her second one. "He was always fussing over me, asking me if I was enjoying myself, refusing beer because he didn't want to drink a lot in front of me, telling his buddies he had to behave himself with his son around. He sure made me feel like a jerk, like I was really cramping his style. He meant well, I guess, but I had a lousy time, and I'm sure he did too."

Becky reached out her hand and gave his arm a sympathetic pat. "The whole thing is crazy. We always had a good time together. My father was a fantastic man. He had this terrific, dry way of saying things, funny without cracking a smile. Why did he have to get killed?" she demanded fiercely.

Tim took hold of her free hand and held it. "You've had it much worse than me. Maybe that's why we're attracted to each other, because we both have troubles."

Becky took her hand away. "I need two hands to eat pizza." She wasn't ready to respond to the meaningful look in his eyes. "Are we attracted to each other?" she asked playfully.

Tim leaned over and rinsed his hands in the river, then stood up. "No, I asked you out because you're so repulsive."

Becky laughed. "Body odor no doubt."

Tim sniffed. "Pollutes the air." He watched her finish her pizza and then took hold of her hand to pull her up. "Come on. These rocks are hard. Let's go back to the car."

"You mean let's go home," she said firmly.

"That depends. . . ."

"On nothing. We're not going to make out in the car."

Tim whistled. "Oh boy, you sure do hang everything out front. Not very subtle."

"I believe in people understanding each other. Here, you take the flashlight. I'll get the pizza box." She picked up the flashlight and handed it to him.

"There are some things you can leave to chance. What if you got in the car and decided it would be nice to kiss me?" He turned on the flashlight and examined her face. "I like the way you look."

"That's nice, thank you. Come on, let's go." Together they got off the rocks and walked up the path.

When they were in the car, without saying a word, Tim put his arms around her and kissed her full on the mouth. She didn't resist, and only smiled at him when he released her. They looked at each other steadily and then they both laughed. As if they had known each other for years, they kissed again. When they were finished, Becky sat back in the seat contentedly. She felt very much at home with Tim; kissing him came as naturally as a kitten takes to milk.

6

She used to love the morning. Becky lay in bed a couple of weeks later remembering. Her mother had been at her best in the morning, the one who was down in the kitchen first, as if each day brought new hope. It was only later when the day had dragged itself out that, perhaps from sheer discouragement, she would withdraw into her shell of despair. But the mornings had been lively. Becky remembered the homely smell of bacon cooking and fresh coffee, of toast or pancakes; of listening to her father singing while he shaved, and then the voices of her parents downstairs, often laughing.

Now each morning she felt she had to readjust all over again to the difference in her life: to remember that her father was dead and her mother in a mental institution. She felt fragmented, as if she were no longer part of a family. She, Nancy, and Stacey were three people living in a house together; but they each seemed to be living separate, private lives held together only by the coincidence of having been born to the same parents. That was not to say that she didn't love them, because she did; but, thinking about it, she realized that for the past few years she and Nancy had not been close. Nancy had gone her way, growing up, keeping her confidences to herself, and not being particularly interested in what Becky was doing. Come to think of it, she knew darn little about what went on in Nancy's head. She knew the surface—that Nancy had preferred starting a career to going to college, that she had had a few romances—but what really went on inside her cool exterior was a mystery. There must be a lot of things she kept to herself.

Stacey was no mystery. She went about her life quite self-sufficiently, arranging to see her friends, watching her TV shows, doing her homework, and only occasionally visibly breaking down into a mood of sadness and despair at the loss of her parents. Yet Becky felt that in her little sister too a lot went on below the surface that she didn't know about.

By the time Becky was fully awake she remembered what was to happen that Saturday: Aunt Marie was coming to visit. Becky's feelings about her aunt were mixed. She wasn't overly fond of her, and yet because she was their father's only sister and the only close relative they had, she felt a family bond. Aunt Marie was a tie to their father and that, Becky thought ruefully, deserved some measure of affection.

"I hope she appreciates what we're doing," Becky said later, as she scrubbed the kitchen floor on her knees. Nancy was ironing curtains, and Stacey was straightening out a hodgepodge of kitchen utensils thrown together in cabinet drawers.

"At least she won't be able to say we're rotten housekeepers," Nancy remarked.

"I wouldn't care if she did," Stacey said.

Becky stood up and surveyed her work. "It is gorgeous. I don't want anyone to walk on it."

"I've got to walk on it," Stacey said from a small pantry where she was perched on a stool. "I want to get out of here."

"You'll have to wait till it dries," Becky told her. "I wish it was Mom coming, not Aunt Marie," she said suddenly. "Then there'd be a point to all this."

"Why don't we go get her?" Stacey asked.

"We can't." Nancy gave Becky a warning look, as if to tell her she shouldn't say things like that in front of Stacey.

"It's stupid not to talk about Mom," Becky said defiantly. "You act as if she's dead," she said to Nancy. "I want to talk about her. I want to talk about Dad too. I want to talk about us. I want to say how I feel. I don't want to just be quiet about everything."

"What good does talking do? It gets everyone upset." Nancy was disturbed by Becky's outburst.

"You're trying to pretend that everything's fine, and we can go on the way we always have. But it isn't, and there's no sense making believe it is." Becky stood barefoot, with her shoes in her hand, staring at the shining floor as if she might find an answer there.

"But there's nothing you can do about any of it," Nancy said. "And there's no reason to change. We just have to go on as we always have."

Becky kept staring at the floor. "That's what's wrong," she said after a few minutes. "I don't want to go on as I always have. Things *are* different. I feel different. There's no one around to tell me what to do— except you," she said to Nancy, "and you're not the same as a parent. I feel that I have to start learning myself what I should do, but I don't know where to start."

"Well, now you'll have Aunt Marie. She'll tell you what to do."

"Thanks a lot. Just what I need!"

"She's going to be here pretty soon. We'd better finish up." Nancy went back to her ironing, and Becky tiptoed across the damp floor.

Aunt Marie arrived in her car with two large suitcases at lunchtime. She was a large woman, built very much like her brother and with the same prominent nose and strong face.

She gave the girls a warm, near-tearful greeting and went upstairs to their parents' bedroom. Becky and Nancy had been close to a fight about where their aunt was going to sleep. Ever since their mother had gone to the hospital, Becky had insisted that the room be left alone, cleaned and ready for their mother, with the door closed. Nancy had argued that that was silly. "In the meantime I could use it to sew in, and we could leave the ironing board up in it. Mom wouldn't care."

"No, it's her room and it should be kept for her," Becky had pleaded. She knew that logic was on Nancy's side; but when Nancy had said that of course Aunt Marie would use that room, Becky felt a betrayal. "Logic isn't everything. You're practical, you always are, but feelings are more important. Mom never cared that much for Aunt Marie, I don't think Dad did either, and she shouldn't be in their room. I can't bear to think of her there."

"And where do you think she's going to sleep?" Nancy had asked.

"She can have my room. I can go in with Stacey and sleep on the floor, or downstairs on the couch. I don't care."

Nancy shook her head. "You can't do that. You need a place to do your homework, and she'd never understand it. Why leave a perfectly good room empty? It's ridiculous. She wouldn't have any privacy in your room— you'd be going in and out all the time to get clothes and books. No, Becky. I let you keep the room unused all this time, but Marie's got to have it."

Becky knew she was licked; and now when she saw her aunt go directly to that room without even asking where she was to stay, she felt a hard knot form in her stomach. Keeping the room unused had been a guarantee for her that her mother would be coming home. Now that good omen was gone.

When Aunt Marie came downstairs she had changed from her traveling dress into a pair of slacks and a shirt. "I took some of your mother's things out of the bureau and put them away in the closet," she announced, "so there'd be drawer space. I don't think she'd mind. Do you expect she'll be coming home?" She sat down at the kitchen table that was set for lunch.

"Of course she's coming home," Becky said briskly. "We just don't know when."

Marie rearranged the cutlery at her place. "I don't believe you can be so sure," she said.

She had been with them five days when the explosion came. It was on Wednesday, after supper, and they were all sitting on the porch when Aunt Marie said that she would like to look at their father's photographs. "He had a lot of old pictures, some of when we were children. I'd like to see them."

Stacey ran into the house and brought back a fat photograph album and a box of loose pictures. "Let's go into the living room where the light is better," Nancy suggested, and the four of them went inside.

Aunt Marie sat down on the sofa with the album in her lap, and the three girls grouped themselves around her. She passed over the photos of the girls as babies and toddlers until she came to pictures of herself and her brother when they were younger. She stopped to look fondly at a snapshot of the girls' father, very handsome in a white suit, standing with a long-haired girl. "That was Martha. We all thought Jim was going to marry her. A lovely girl. I sure was surprised when he let her get away. Fancy her picture being here!"

Becky bristled. "Dad used to say Mom was his first and last love. He never wanted to marry anyone else."

Their aunt laughed. "Well, maybe. But the girls ran after him. I never expected him to settle down."

"Our father was very domestic, he loved his home and his family," Nancy said.

"Sure, but he liked to go out too. More than your mother did, I think."

"We used to go a lot of places," Stacey put in. "We had beautiful picnics."

"I mean theater, opera, resorts. Your father used to like excitement, people."

"Here's a picture of you and my father," Stacey said, pointing to a snapshot of Aunt Marie and their father in shorts on the dock of a lake.

"Oh, my." She held the album up to the light to examine the faded photograph. "You girls won't mind if I take this. I'd like to have it." She started to take the picture out of the album.

"This album belongs to Mom," Becky said. "I don't think you should take anything without asking her."

"That's true," Nancy said, nodding her head in agreement.

"But it's a picture of me. And my own brother. Your mother won't care. And besides . . ." Aunt Marie didn't finish the sentence, but her meaning was clear.

Becky knew full well what her aunt was implying, but she asked quietly, "Besides what?"

Aunt Marie shrugged. "Even if Margaret ever does come home, I don't think she's going to care about an old picture."

"It may be exactly what she *will* care about," Becky said. "An old picture of my father may mean a great deal to her—we don't know. But you seem to be so sure she's not coming home."

Their aunt flushed. "I never said that. But from what I hear it seems quite unlikely."

"What do you hear?" Nancy asked in surprise.

Marie was embarrassed. "Maybe not exactly hear, but I'm not stupid, you know. I saw how she was when I was here after the funeral, and knowing what she tried to do to herself . . . a friend of mine had a relative very much the same. . . ."

"I don't want to hear about your friend's relative," Becky said in a tired voice. She took the album out of Aunt Marie's hands. "When Mom comes home we can ask her, and she can send you the picture if she wants."

"Well of all . . ." Marie was almost speechless. "I always told your father he was too easy on you girls, you especially, Becky. Many a time you could have

70

used a good spanking, always being so uppity and wanting your own way. He called it independence, but I can give it a better name."

"Please don't," Becky said with a small smile.

"I'm not surprised your mother had a nervous breakdown, with your father gone, trying to cope with you." She leaned back in her chair and made a gesture of helplessness that was incongruous with her large frame and strong features. "I was thinking of offering to come here and help you girls out, but I don't think I could do it. I'd like to help, you're my only brother's children and the only close kin I have in this world, but it'd be too much for me. Just Nancy and Stacey would be all right, Nancy can take care of herself anyway. But not you, Becky. I'd land in the nuthouse myself."

"I don't need anyone to take care of me," Becky said haughtily. "I'm perfectly capable of taking care of myself."

It was still early in the evening, and Becky took a sweater from the hall closet, called out that she was going for a walk, and left the house. She was more upset than she wanted to admit, even to herself. Although she knew she shouldn't care what her aunt had to say, she felt hurt, and she was angry with both herself and Marie that she had gotten into such a state. She hated being unable to control her feelings. She didn't think she was a bad person. Maybe she was thoughtless, perhaps even rude; but she didn't mean to be.

Becky walked with no idea of where she was going. It didn't take long for her eyes to get accustomed to the dark, and it seemed to her that she walked several miles before she calmed down. When she saw the sign

71

for a small hamburger and coffee shop, she went inside and ordered a cup of coffee and a doughnut, glad that she had picked up her wallet on the way out. She was in a neighborhood she rarely frequented. It was an old working-class section of town near the railroad tracks and an abandoned railroad station.

As she sat drinking her coffee, she kept staring at a sign behind the counter that said "Help Wanted." Idly she asked the waitress what the job was. "We need someone to help out. Wash dishes, clean up the tables, mop the floor. How old are you?" The young woman brushed her hair away from her face with her hand and studied her.

"Sixteen," Becky said glibly. "I'll be seventeen soon."

"Come around during the day when the boss is here," the girl told her, and poured a cup of coffee for a sallow-faced man sitting at the counter. "It's not much of a job, but the boss is okay. Want anything else? More coffee?"

"No, thank you. Maybe I'll see you tomorrow." Becky paid her check and went out. A job. Maybe that would solve everything. She was sick of having to ask Nancy for money—if a kid didn't have any parents, she should have the option of taking care of herself. Having her own money would be a help at home. The more Becky thought about it, the more appealing the idea was. Nancy would respect her for getting a job, and it would show she was responsible. If she had enough money she could even leave home. For a few minutes Becky felt elated by the idea. She felt an overwhelming need to take control of her life, and a job could be the first step.

When Becky got home, Stacey had gone to bed and Nancy and Aunt Marie were sitting on the porch. She hesitated, but Nancy called out to her to come out. Aunt Marie was silent.

"I'm sorry I was rude," Becky said to her aunt. "I didn't mean to be."

Marie seemed surprised but also at a loss as to how to accept the apology gracefully. She simply waved her hand, dismissing the whole episode as something she did not care to talk about.

Becky sat with them a short while, saying little. Her mind was on the possibility of the job. It was a nothing kind of job, yet the rather shabby place had appealed to her. It was clean, and the girl working there was pleasant and attractive. Also, she had said the boss was all right. The idea of a job and money of her own was exciting, but Becky wasn't going to talk about it until she really had it. She soon said good night and went up to bed.

7

It wasn't until Friday afternoon that Becky was able to go back to the hamburger place. Concentrating on her school work during the week had been difficult. Many of the kids called their school the jailhouse, and Becky had felt the same that week: imprisoned when she wanted to be out free. In her English class she had been busily trying to figure out how much money she could make over the summer when her teacher, Mrs. Warner, called on her to answer a question about the irony in Edith Wharton's book *Ethan Frome*. Becky looked up with a blank face.

"I didn't think you were paying attention," Mrs. Warner said, and called on someone else to answer. When the class was dismissed she asked Becky to stay. "What's the matter? I can usually count on you, but lately I've noticed your mind has been far away from the classroom."

"I know. I have a lot of things on my mind," Becky told her.

Mrs. Warner was a pleasant-faced, youngish woman

74

and she spoke in a quiet voice. "I know that this has been a hard year for you. But I don't like to see it affect your work. How are you and your sisters getting along at home?" She looked at Becky sympathetically.

"So-so. I guess we're managing okay." Becky was tempted to tell her that maybe she wasn't coming back to school next year. If she was sixteen and working, she wouldn't have to. But she decided that would only let her in for a lecture, and she didn't feel like listening to one. Besides, she didn't know yet if she had the job, or what would be happening by next year.

"Don't let your schoolwork slip," Mrs. Warner said. "You'll be the sorry one in the end."

"Yes, thank you," Becky said politely, and left.

At least she didn't have to go home to be with Aunt Marie that afternoon. All week Becky had gone out of her way to be nice to her aunt. She had gone right home from school, and had taken her out shopping a few times. But it had been with a sigh of relief that she had said good-bye to her that morning.

Becky headed toward the other side of town when she got to the village. In the light of day she could see that the coffee shop was in a neat but poor neighborhood. The patches of ground in front of the houses did not have much in the way of lawn, and the houses were in need of painting. She passed a couple of old men sitting on a porch, drinking beer in their rocking chairs.

The waitress who had been there Wednesday evening was nowhere in sight; behind the counter was a chubby, middle-aged man with a tired, gray face. When he looked up at Becky she saw that his eyes were deep set and alert.

"I came about the job," Becky said, indicating the sign. "Is it still open?"

75

"Yes, it's open." He looked her up and down, making Becky feel self-conscious. "I don't think you'd like it."

"I know what it is. At least I think so. I was here a few nights ago and the girl told me. I don't mind mopping floors and washing dishes. I do it at home all the time." She gave him a bright smile. "At least here I'd get paid for it."

"Not much," the man said. "How old are you?"

"Sixteen," Becky said promptly.

The man shrugged. "With this kind of job you don't have to lie about your age. But if you say you're sixteen, it's okay with me. You go to school?"

"Yes. I thought I could start coming in after school and on Saturdays, and when school's out in June I could work full time."

The man gave a slow smile. "You got it all figured out. Why do you want a job like this so bad?"

"I need money," she said simply.

He studied her again. "You don't look like you're so hard up. Your mother know you want to come to work here?"

"I haven't got a mother," Becky said. She was not going to go into her personal life with him.

The man shrugged again. "That's too bad. If you want to try it it's okay with me." He told her what the salary was, and as he had said, it wasn't much; but Becky felt pleased. When he told her to start on Monday, Becky thanked him and left quickly before he could change his mind.

On the way home Becky's mind was filled with figures. She kept adding up dollars and cents—so many weeks after school, so many Saturdays, so many weeks during vacation. It was hard to do it in her head, but she was impressed with the approximate amount she could earn by the end of the summer. If she saved it all, she could have eight or nine hundred dollars. That was a heady thought.

Becky went home the long way around, through the village; and as she had hoped, she saw Tim. He was carrying groceries to a customer's car. "Is this a late afternoon, or an early one?" she asked after he had deposited the bags of groceries.

He looked at his watch. "I get off in half an hour. What's up?"

"I feel like celebrating. I just got a job."

"Wow. What?"

Becky told him where she was going to work but quickly glossed over what she would be doing.

"Is it a decent place?" Tim asked.

"Nothing fancy," she said airily. "But it's okay. The owner seems nice."

"Lots of luck. How do you want to celebrate?"

"I don't know. Come over to the house when you're finished."

"If you hang around I'll drive you home."

"Okay. I'll meet you back here in half an hour."

Becky wandered around the village. She went into the dime store where she bought a box of crayons for Stacey and considered and rejected mascara for herself; then into the shop that had newspapers and magazines, which she decided all looked junky. Besides, she wasn't going to waste her money. Money was still very much on her mind, and she kept wondering when they would hear something about their case. She knew Nancy was in touch with David Cimino, but all she could get out of her sister was that David had spoken to the factory's lawyers and so far they had not met. She never used to think about money. She knew that her father hadn't made much, but they always had the things that were needed: sufficient clothes, a new roof when the old one leaked, plenty of food, and small but adequate allowances for the girls. When Nancy had decided to go to work instead of trying for college, their father had been disappointed but, as he had said, not surprised. "She's going to get married young anyway; but not you, Becky. You have the drive and the brains for a profession. You can be a lawyer, a doctor; you pick it and I'll see that there's the money for it."

Now college seemed remote, and Becky was too concerned with the present, still too emotionally upset by the events of the past year, to project into the distant future. She felt, however, that she was groping toward a goal and that someday she would fulfill her father's hopes for her. She wasn't sure what she would end up doing. She didn't think she wanted to be a lawyer or a doctor, but maybe she would have a career in business. Perhaps she would take business courses. Right now she was worried about where their money was going to come from. They were still getting workmen's compensation and some money from the life-insurance policy their father had. But the insurance money would run out and the compensation check alone wasn't enough. What if their lawsuit didn't get settled? What would happen to them?

Becky had started saving her money. She felt silly doing it because she had so little, just what she made baby-sitting and sometimes cleaning someone's house or washing a car, and in the summer mowing lawns.

But watching her small savings grow gave her a good feeling about herself, as if somewhere hidden within her bewilderment and anger there was a nodule of determination and sanity.

A little more than half an hour later she went back to meet Tim, who was waiting outside the store. They walked to his car. As always when she first saw Tim, she reacted anew to his presence. He didn't hang loose the way other boys his age did. He had a compact strength, as if he had been put together to last. Durability, that was it. Tim wasn't going to break easily. Becky, who was always comparing herself to other people, felt that she had some of that strength too, physically. But she didn't have it emotionally. I'm like a pretzel, she thought, all wound around myself instead of going in a straight line.

Tim had a quart of ice cream with him. "This is all I could find for a celebration," he said. "Maple nut, hope you like it."

"My favorite. Let's go home and eat it. Come on."

Becky's house was empty. There was a note from Stacey saying she was at a friend's house, and it was too early for Nancy to be home from work. Becky got out plates for the ice cream and looked in the refrigerator to see if there was any chocolate sauce. She couldn't find sauce, but there was a beautiful chocolate cake.

"Look what I found." Becky took the cake out. "Just what we need for our party."

"Do you think it's all right to eat it?" Tim asked.

"Why not? What's a cake for if not to be eaten? Nancy didn't mention any company. She probably made it for the weekend, so we'll eat my share now." She cut off a generous slice for Tim and one for herself.

They sat down at the kitchen table and had a feast. After they had eaten second helpings of the cake and finished about half the quart of ice cream, Becky sat back with a sigh of contentment.

"What do you want to do now?" Tim asked.

"Let's go for a ride. Have you got time?"

Tim grinned. "For you, always."

"Where do you want to go?" Tim asked after they had driven through the village.

"I don't care. Somewhere where we can drive fast. Real fast, a hundred miles an hour." She didn't look at him when she spoke, but stared out of the window.

"Cool it, kid. I'm not driving any hundred miles an hour. Seventy-five's about all this car can do, anyway. Besides, if you want to commit suicide, do it alone. Count me out."

She turned toward him with an angelic smile. "Wouldn't it be romantic? Teenage couple drive over cliff in suicide pact. Can't you just see the headlines? We'd be famous."

"But dead. Very dead. And we'd never know. We might just get a tiny paragraph on the last page," Tim replied.

"Have you ever wanted to die?" she asked abruptly, in a serious voice.

"No, never. And what's more, I don't intend to. I plan to be an exception to the rule."

Becky laughed. "That's nice. I like that. And maybe you will be, who knows. Let's go over to the falls and walk in the woods. Violets may be coming up."

Tim looked at her in amazement. "One minute it's driving a hundred miles an hour and the next it's looking for violets. I can't keep up with you."

"Don't you ever feel like doing something crazy?"

"I guess not the way you do. You really scared me that night when you were standing on that rock. I thought for a second you were going to jump in."

"Would you have cared?" she asked lightly.

He flashed her a look revealing an intensity of feeling that made her heart skip. "Yes," he said soberly. "I would have cared."

After Tim parked the car they walked on a dirt path that followed the river toward the falls. The path was narrow, but Tim took hold of Becky's hand so that they walked side by side. "I wonder if there are fish in this stream," he said.

"I suppose you're thinking of some fantastic ways to cook fish. Do you always think of food and cooking?"

"Sometimes I think about other things. Right now I'm thinking we should climb down to the water and sit on that rock that juts out." They walked off the path down an incline to the water. But instead of going to the rock Tim led her over to a plot of soft moss and they sat there. Becky stretched out on her back with her arms under her head and looked up at the sky. Tim sat beside her, hugging his knees.

"What are you thinking of?" he asked.

"How peaceful it is here. I could stay forever."

"You'd get lonesome," Tim said.

"I'm used to being lonesome. I've been lonesome for months now. Ever since my father was killed. God, I miss him."

"He must have been quite a guy. You must miss your mother too." Tim looked at her sympathetically and touched her hair gently.

"Not in the same way. Of course I miss her, but she

was closer to Nancy. I was closer to my father. I think about him so much."

"Maybe too much. I don't mean you should forget about him, but you have to get over feeling so badly."

"I never will. You wouldn't understand."

"Don't say that," Tim said sharply. "Why wouldn't I understand? I miss having a father who's close. Don't you think boys have feelings? I'm sick of girls thinking they're the only ones who are sensitive, who have emotions. That's so much rot."

"Don't scream at me."

"I'm not screaming." Suddenly he bent down and kissed her full and hard on her mouth. He stretched out alongside her and held her close against him. "I have a lot of feelings," Tim said softly. "I hope you understand."

She didn't answer but lay quietly in his arms. His body felt strong and hard against her, and his ironed shirt had a clean smell to it. She closed her eyes and wondered what it would be like if she gave in to what she knew he wanted. Suddenly her loneliness, her own yearnings over the past year, and her desperate need of solace seemed centered in her body. To just relax and let whatever could happen, happen might be the answer— She lay very still, and let him stroke her hair and kiss her mouth and her throat, unbutton the top button of her blouse. The setting was perfect; a small glen safely away from the path and shielded by trees. Then she drew away.

"Don't do that," Tim whispered.

"I have to," Becky said, and sat up.

"Why? You want it as much as I do. You know you're not a cold fish. We care about each other. It's not going to hurt anyone. You want to be independent, so be it." He sat up too, and faced her.

"That's one reason why I can't," she said simply. "Don't you see? If you and I had sex now I would feel I wasn't being responsible. I'd feel that Nancy's telling me all the time I can't take care of myself would be true. I don't want to do anything that would make me feel ashamed, or cheap, afterwards."

Tim bristled. "There's nothing to be ashamed of if two people care about each other; and you're not cheap, either. If you're going to run your life to please Nancy, you'll never be independent."

Becky picked at a thread in her jeans. "It's not to please Nancy," she said in a low voice. "I want to feel strong, independent of everyone, including you." She gave him a small smile. "I don't want to be pushed into anything. I'm not ready for sex. I have too many things to straighten out in my own mind and with my own feelings."

Tim stood up. "Okay, you win. Let's go."

Becky gave him an angry look. "Is that the only reason you came here? To have sex? You're disgusting."

"Don't you dare call me that. You're the one who says that sex is cheap. I don't think so. If we stay here we're only going to fight, so we may as well go."

"Yes, we may as well," Becky said coldly. She ignored the hand he held out to her and scrambled to her feet.

They walked back to the car without speaking. Becky slammed the door closed after she got in. Tim stepped on the gas too hard and started the car with a jolt that threw Becky forward against the dashboard. "You don't have to kill me," she snapped.

Tim turned around to see that she was all right, and continued driving; but he slowed down. "I don't know what you're mad about," he said, "I'm the one who was rejected."

"You poor thing. I really feel sorry for you."

"Don't get sarcastic. I hate sarcasm."

"Too bad. Listen, you told me not to run my life to please Nancy. Well, I'm not running it to please you either."

"You sure aren't. There are some people who are civil just to please themselves."

Becky couldn't think of an answer so she kept quiet. She was trying to tell herself that Tim was a gross boy she didn't care about, but when she glanced across at him she knew that wasn't so. His sensitive face looked miserable, and she had to control herself to keep from putting her arms around him and saying that she was sorry.

When they got to her house, Becky sat for a minute before getting out, hoping he would say something. When he remained silent, she opened the car door, and then felt his hand on her arm. "Let's not leave each other mad," Tim said.

"Who's mad?"

Grinning, Tim turned and looked around the back of the car. "Don't see a soul. Must be two other people."

"Must be." Becky grinned too. "See you."

"Soon. Very soon," Tim said, and drove off.

Nancy and Stacey were both home when Becky went inside. The minute she walked into the kitchen and saw Nancy's face dark with anger, she knew something was wrong. "What's the matter?" she asked.

"You're a fine one to ask. My cake," Nancy wailed. "It's a mess. How could you, Becky? You might have asked me before you ate up half of it."

"You weren't home to ask. Besides, since when do I need your permission to eat some cake in my own home in my own fridge? That is really too much."

Nancy whirled around from the counter where she was mixing herbs for a meat loaf. "But this was special. I made it for tonight. David's coming for dinner."

Becky looked contrite. "Oh, I am sorry. But how was I to know? You didn't say anything."

"I don't have to report everything to you, do I? Anyway, I forgot to mention it. But it seems to me that if you saw a whole cake like this you could figure out that maybe I had made it for a reason." Nancy shook her head despairingly. "I can't serve this thing. It looks awful."

"Of course you can serve it. We'll put it on plates in here. Tim brought some ice cream; we can put a blob on each serving and it will look great."

"I suppose so," Nancy said grudgingly. "So Tim was here with you?"

"Yes, Tim was here with me." Becky looked at her sister defiantly. "And if I have to get permission from you about what I'm allowed to eat, that's the end. You could have at least left a note saying you wanted to save your precious cake. Believe me, I wouldn't have touched it."

Saying that, she walked out of the kitchen. She felt discouraged and depressed. Up in her room she realized she hadn't even told Nancy about the job. She knew her sister would put it down. Thinking about it herself now, it didn't sound like anything to get elated about. She sat down at her desk, her chin cupped in her hands. Having a fight with Tim hadn't helped. But she wished she could think of some way to get out of the situation she was in. She couldn't do anything about her mother's illness, and she had to accept her father's death; but she didn't have to accept living with Nancy. If only she could find a way to be on her own. . . .

She tried to think of herself as someone separate, but what kind of a person was she? Was she responsible, could she take care of herself? Suddenly she was intensely curious about herself. She knew she was stronger than Nancy. Behind Nancy's cool efficiency Becky was beginning to suspect a backlog of pent-up anger that was doing her sister no good. She wondered if Nancy could ever let go and just enjoy herself. As for herself, she knew she was someone with a streak of adventure, willing to take risks, but on the whole sensible enough to stay away from danger. She had proven that to herself this afternoon. Becky surveyed herself in the mirror and decided she wasn't so bad.

8

Becky stayed up in her room when she heard David's car pull into the driveway. She called to Stacey to do the same. "Why can't we go down?" Stacey asked, coming in to see Becky.

"We can, in a few minutes. I think Nancy might want to be alone with him first."

Stacey grinned. "Is he her boyfriend?"

"I think maybe he's getting to be. I think she likes him."

"He's good looking, except for his beard. It must feel funny to kiss someone with a mustache and a beard."

"I don't think so. If you kiss on the mouth it wouldn't matter." Becky giggled. "Unless the mustache is very long."

"Do you kiss boys on the mouth?" Stacey asked.

"Sometimes. If I like a boy a lot. But the boys I know don't have mustaches or beards. Not yet. I don't think they even shave. Maybe Tim does once in a while." Becky brushed her hair to get ready to go downstairs.

"Is Tim your boyfriend?"

"I don't know. We're friends." Becky studied her

reflection in the mirror. Maybe Tim was her boyfriend, although it was something neither of them had said in so many words. She wondered how he felt about her after what had happened down by the river. He seemed to understand and accept her reasons.

Becky felt shy with David. She remembered the big, shabby but impressive office and that David was a lawyer. But there wasn't anything stuffy about him. He sat on the floor and played a card game with Stacey; he insisted on helping to carry plates and food into the dining room; and he kept looking at Nancy unabashedly. Becky was sure they were both falling in love.

After dinner was finished and the table was cleared, David became serious. They were still sitting at the round dining-room table. "I don't like talking business after such a scrumptious meal," David said, "but there are a few things we should decide on. It would be helpful if we could know just what the prognosis for your mother is." He spoke hesitantly. "If she is going to be well enough to come home and to function, that is one thing; but if it turns out that she is incapacitated, the court will want to appoint a guardian for you two," he said, turning to Becky and Stacey. "You will need someone to protect your interests."

"I thought that's what you were doing," Becky said. "At least as far as our case is concerned."

"I am. I am representing all of you; but if your mother is out of the picture, as minors you will have to have a guardian. Nancy could legally become your guardian if your mother is not able, but that would have to be determined."

"Nancy, our guardian?" Becky was shocked. "She's

only a few years older than I am. She can't be my guardian."

"I told you Becky wouldn't like that," Nancy said.

"No, I wouldn't. It doesn't make sense to me." The very idea was ridiculous to Becky.

"It's really just a legal term," David said gently. "It means she can sign an agreement, speak for you in court. She wouldn't do anything you didn't know about or that you didn't agree to."

"How do I know? It isn't that I don't trust Nancy. I do. It's the *idea* of it. I don't want Nancy to be my guardian. It would be impossible...." Becky didn't want to say it, but deep down she was afraid Nancy might take advantage of her if she were Becky's guardian. Now, without a formal label, Nancy was telling her what to do, wanting to be in control of how things should be done. If it were made legal, there'd be no stopping her. The more Becky thought about it, the more impossible the idea became.

"Well, we don't have to decide now," David said amiably. "First we'll have to try to get some information from your mother's doctor and know what the situation there is."

In a short while Becky excused herself to go upstairs and motioned to Stacey to do the same. They left Nancy and David together on the porch. When she said good night to David, Becky had a sudden, strong premonition that she was speaking to her future brother-in-law. The thought hit her with such a certainty that she almost kissed him good night; but she thought better of doing that.

Becky was still wide awake when she heard David's car pull out of the driveway and her sister come upstairs. She called to Nancy to come into her room.

"It's so late," Nancy protested.

"I know, but we never have time to talk. I've got something to tell you—I've got a job."

Nancy had come into her room and was sitting on the edge of the bed. Becky sat up and propped herself against the pillows. "It's not much of a job but it's a job," Becky said. She told her briefly where she was going to work and emphasized how nice Mr. Kowalski, her boss, was. "You won't have to give me money anymore. I'll be able to buy my own lunches and clothes and have my own spending money. I can probably save some too."

Nancy looked dubious. "It's not a good neighborhood. I don't know why you want a job like that anyway. You'll be getting only the minimum wage, so the money isn't going to make that much difference. Cleaning women get more than that."

"I knew you'd put it down," Becky said disconsolately. "I was hoping you wouldn't, that at least you'd think I was doing something constructive."

"I don't see anything constructive about working in a dinky coffee shop clearing tables and mopping floors." Nancy's face had a look of disgust.

"It's a perfectly good, clean place. As far as you're concerned, I never do anything right. It's only a start, my first steady job; you could at least be encouraging."

Becky thought again about her father. He was the only one who had made her feel terrific, a person who was going to be somebody, who could do anything she made up her mind to. She said something to that effect to Nancy, who flashed her eyes at her. "Sure," Nancy said, "Dad was always building you up. He didn't even care when I decided not to go to college."

"But that was your decision. You could have gone; he said it was up to you." It wasn't fair for Nancy to blame their father for that.

"I know it was my decision. But maybe if he had encouraged me more . . . "

"That's not fair. Besides, you're doing marvelously in your job. You like it and you're getting ahead—what are you complaining about?"

"I'm not complaining," Nancy said impatiently. "Anyway it's too late now. But I don't see why you need a job. You have enough to do with your school-work and helping here in the house. Right now I'm managing with the money. You could spend some afternoons with Stacey."

"Stacey has her own friends. She's hardly ever home after school."

"Maybe she should be home. Who knows where she is."

"I know. She tells me where she's going or she leaves a note. You keep trying to make me out to be someone irresponsible, and I'm not. I wish you'd get that through your head."

Nancy sighed. "You're too inconsistent. Sometimes you're sensible and a lot of times you're not."

Becky gave a rueful laugh. "Thank goodness for that. I'd hate to be sensible all the time." Like you, she thought, uptight and critical. "Are you in love with David?" she asked, changing the subject.

Nancy looked startled and about to take offense at the question, but then apparently changed her mind. "I'm not sure. I think maybe I am. I feel very comfortable with him. Do you like him?"

Becky nodded. "Yes, I do. I think you two are going to get married."

"Oh, Becky." Nancy blushed. "You're rushing things. He's ten years older than I am."

"So what? That's not much. I think he's in love with you. I have a feeling you're going to get married—I felt it the first time I saw you two together."

"You're crazy," Nancy said, but she didn't look unhappy about the prospect.

After Nancy had said good night and Becky settled back under the covers, she continued to think about the possibility of Nancy's getting married. Where would that leave her and Stacey? Conceivably Stacey could live with Nancy and David, but for her to stay with them would be impossible. It wouldn't be fair to them, a newly married couple, to have someone her age around; and she definitely would not want it. Having Stacey would be enough for a new marriage. She would have to get out. But how, and where?

As the days went on, Becky felt that soon, soon she would settle down into a routine, that her life would go back to being the same as it was before her father's death and her mother's illness. On the outside her life wasn't that different: she went to school, tried to pay attention in her English and math classes, hated biology, played basketball, spent time in the library, and complained about too much homework. The afternoons were different. Instead of spending time with Lisa or some of the other girls, she went to Mr. Kowalski's coffee shop to work. Soon that too fell into a routine, but one that she quite enjoyed. She liked talking to the customers. Some of the same people came in daily, and some of them ate the same thing every time: Mrs. Reilly had black coffee and a western, talked to them in her rich Irish voice, and said she shouldn't eat pie but often did. Mr. Levine from the tailor shop had a bowl of soup, even on the hottest day, buttered toast, and a glass of tea. He was one of Becky's favorites, a man with a sad face and bright eyes, who told Becky that one day he would bring in his collection of pictures of the Great Depression to show her. "No one remembers what it was like in the thirties," he said often, "but I have a record."

It was inside that she felt unsettled, somehow as if she were sitting on a geological fault waiting for the earthquake to begin. Each morning she woke up expectantly—today SOMETHING was going to happen: they would get some word about their mother, Nancy would come home with news from David about their case, Tim would say that he loved her, she would figure out a way to leave home and live by herself, they would suddenly be rich. . . .

Just before school was out in June something did happen, but it wasn't what Becky was looking for. She had gone to meet Nancy at the store because they were going to do some shopping before they went home. Becky was trying on shoes when Nancy said, "Don't spend too much money. You're going to have to quit your job when school is out."

Becky looked at her sister in amazement. "Why on earth should I quit my job?"

"Because of Stacey. She can't be left home alone all day. You'll have to be there."

It took a while for Becky to digest that. She lost interest in the shoes, a pretty pair of beige sandals, and decided she didn't feel like buying anything. "Let's go home. I don't feel like shopping anymore." Becky felt stunned and depressed, and she wanted to think about what to do. She had to agree that Stacey couldn't be left alone all day, but she didn't think it was fair for her to have to stay home. There had to be another way. . . .

"I just want to stop and pick up some stockings," Nancy said. In the car Becky was silent, and Nancy eyed her unhappy face uncomfortably. "Staying home in the summer isn't so terrible. That coffee shop will probably be hot and awful anyway."

"Mr. Kowalski has an air conditioner," Becky said colorlessly.

"Well for heaven's sake don't look as if you're about to be hanged."

"Pardon me for not getting up and cheering." Becky threw her sister a baleful glance.

Stacey was waiting for them at home. She took one look at their faces and made a grimace. "What's eating you two? Did something happen?" she asked with a worried look.

They both knew she was thinking about their mother. "No, nothing happened," Becky assured her.

"I told Becky she had to quit her job to stay home with you this summer. You'd think I'd sentenced her to a year in prison." Nancy started getting supper ready. "You want to chop these vegetables?" She handed some onions, celery, and carrots to Becky. "Make them pretty fine, please."

"Yes, ma'am."

"I can take care of myself," Stacey said. "She doesn't have to baby-sit for me. I'm almost ten years old, I'm not a baby."

"You're not going to stay home alone here every

day. You won't be ten until November." Nancy's voice was very firm.

"She's right," Becky said.

Stacey laughed. "I can't believe you two are agreeing. So what's the problem?"

"There is no problem," Becky said curtly.

Becky made little effort to hide her disappointment, and the three girls sat through a strained supper. "I'm sorry," Becky said when she got up to clear the table, "but I can't pretend I'm happy when I'm not."

"That's all right," Stacey said consolingly. "You didn't cry."

Becky gave her a grateful smile. "No, I didn't cry."

After supper she went over to Lisa's house. As usual Lisa's mother greeted her warmly. "You're such a stranger, you hardly ever come over anymore."

"Because of my job, but that's going to be over with," Becky said gloomily. Then she poured out her story to Lisa and her parents.

"It's a shame," Mrs. Slovak said sympathetically, "that you girls are without a mother or a father. A terrible thing."

"We get along pretty well," Becky said defensively. "I hate disappointing Mr. Kowalski. He's been so nice to me."

"Isn't there a day-care camp your sister could go to?" Mr. Slovak asked.

"Yes, there is," Lisa said eagerly. "I know there is. That's what you have to do, Becky."

Becky's hopes were raised, but only for a moment. "That'll be expensive, won't it?"

"It's for working mothers," Mr. Slovak said. "I don't see why it couldn't be for working sisters as well. You should look into it."

Becky went home feeling excited, but she didn't say anything. She was going to find out more before she talked to Nancy and Stacey.

The next day in school Lisa gave Becky the name and address of the day-care camp, and on Saturday the two girls went to meet the director. Becky told Nancy she was going out with Lisa after work but she didn't say where. The place was on the outskirts of New Salem, and the girls took a bus and then walked the rest of the way.

The director turned out to be two people, a middle-aged couple who lived in a small house set in a wooded lot of hemlocks and birches. Becky noticed a lot of outdoor play equipment around, and in back a nice-sized pond. Mr. and Mrs. Thompson seemed surprised to see two young girls keeping the appointment, but led them into a neat office in the house.

Becky introduced herself and Lisa, and quickly explained why she had come. "But do you have the authority to enroll your sister in the camp?" Mr. Thompson asked, and shook his head dubiously. "I'm not saying we can't take her, but I think we need to deal with an adult."

"If I knew she would be accepted, my sister could make the arrangements. I'd like to know how much it would cost, first." Becky looked from one to the other.

"I think we'd better discuss that with your sister," Mrs. Thompson said kindly. "We have some state funds, and it will depend on her income and the family situation. Your sister may be eligible for a partial scholarship."

Becky realized that she wasn't going to get anything

definite from them, and the girls soon left. Once outside, Becky gave vent to her feeling of frustration. "As if they couldn't tell us how much it would be. I could have told them anything they wanted to know. It gets me so mad to be treated like a kid now. Nancy is no more of an adult than I am. Just because she's a few years older she's treated differently and can do anything she wants."

Becky stormed away until they got on the bus. Then she turned to Lisa with a grin. "Thanks for listening, I had to get that off my chest."

"I don't blame you. It doesn't seem fair."

Stacey received the news of going to a day camp enthusiastically, but Nancy was more restrained. David was at the house that evening when Becky told them her idea. He and Nancy seemed to have a standing Saturday-night date; either they would go out to dinner or he would eat at home with them. That night they were eating in and going to a late movie.

"It sounds like a good idea," David said at the supper table. "Don't you think so?" he asked Nancy.

"I'd like to see the camp first," Nancy said. Then, turning to Becky, she added, "You might have asked me to go with you."

"I thought I'd check it out first," Becky said. "Lisa and I thought it looked great. A lot of equipment and a pond. The Thompsons seemed very nice. I think Stacey would have a fantastic summer."

"You mean you'd get what you want," Nancy said with a rueful smile.

"Is there anything wrong with that?" Becky asked, looking at her sister innocently.

Nancy had to laugh with the others. "You're quite a manager."

"I accept the compliment," Becky said with a grin, knowing full well Nancy had not intended it as such.

It was about a week before Nancy found time to visit the Thompsons and look over the camp. Apparently she was satisfied, because she came home one night and quietly announced that Stacey was accepted and would go when school was out.

Becky threw her arms around her sister and thanked her. Nancy disentangled herself from Becky's onslaught and said that she still didn't know what Becky found so great in that job of hers. She hugged Becky affectionately, however, and went away humming.

Becky was sure David had talked Nancy into enrolling Stacey, and she thought she saw signs of his influence on her in other instances: a few nights before she hadn't bawled Becky out for leaving dirty dishes in the sink; then Nancy had come home with a wild strapless summer dress she'd bought at an expensive shop; and, wonder of wonders, when Mrs. Marsh had come noseying around, Nancy had told her politely but firmly to mind her own business.

9

By late June school was out, Stacey was settled in the camp, and Becky faced an uneventful summer of full-time work. Yet she still felt unsettled and as if she was on the verge of some turn in her life. She put it down to wishful thinking, but she clung to the hope nevertheless.

To break the monotony and to start off the summer, she and Lisa decided to have a party. "Your house?" Lisa asked.

"Sure. When Nancy isn't home. I think she and David are going to a dinner theater next Saturday night. I'll find out."

Later, after supper, Becky casually asked Nancy what show she and David were going to see the following Saturday.

Nancy named a musical comedy, and, still casual, Becky said, "I'm going to ask some of the kids over."

"Just don't have a big crowd," Nancy said.

Becky's immediate thought was "so what if I did?" but she kept her mouth shut. The next day she called Lisa from the shop and told her to go ahead and invite people. She stopped at her friend's house after work and found that Lisa and her mother had everything planned. "You're working," Mrs. Slovak said, "and you have enough trouble. I'm glad you're having a party, Becky. It's time you had a little fun."

Becky was well aware that even the thought of having a party was a big thing for her; it would be the first since her father's death. He had liked parties, and she felt he would be happy for her. Mrs. Slovak had volunteered to make pizzas, so the two girls went over the guest list and decided how many she should make. Lisa said she would bake brownies, and they agreed to ask some of the boys to bring soda. Becky left feeling cheerful.

Saturday night Lisa and Becky were getting everything set up for their party when David came to pick up Nancy. "Boy, this looks good," David said, eyeing the pizzas, cookies, and brownies set out on the table. "Maybe we should stay home," he said to Nancy.

"We probably should," Nancy said. "I'm not crazy about going out and leaving these kids here."

"Oh, for God's sake, Nancy, we're *not* kids. We don't need a chaperon. Have a good time and don't worry about us."

The party started off well. Tim came early to help, but there was nothing to do except sit around and wait for the others. Their friends from school came in a group a little later, and then, with Becky's stereo playing downstairs in the living room, the party took off. Around ten-thirty four boys came over with their own instruments, and soon a guitar, saxophone, electric piano, and drum were beating out the tunes. Stacey came downstairs because she wanted to "watch" the music, and Becky let her stay.

Everything was going well, and everyone seemed to be having a good time. The girls brought out the food around eleven o'clock and were just passing around the hot pizza slices when two boys and a girl came in with six-packs of beer. Becky knew the three slightly from school.

"Seems we came at the right time," the taller of the two boys said, glancing at the food. Although Becky hadn't invited them, she didn't know how to say that they weren't welcome.

"I don't know if we have enough food for extras," she said hesitatingly, thinking she was being as diplomatic as possible.

"That's all right," said the same tall boy, "we don't eat much and we brought our own beer." His name was Doug Fielding, and he gave Becky a grin.

"I guess you did," she answered. He reeked of beer.

Tim came over and stood beside Becky. "This is a private party," he said quietly. "Perhaps you'd better drink your beer someplace else."

"No, we like it here. Come on." He motioned to his two friends, who had been standing in the doorway.

Tim was about to stop them, but Becky took hold of his arm. "No, I don't want a fight. Maybe they'll eat some food and leave. They're only kids from school, they won't do anything."

"They've been drinking a lot of beer," Tim said.

In less than ten minutes Becky was wishing desperately that she had gotten some of the boys to help Tim get rid of the three right away. After Doug and his two friends were inside, they went to the table and Doug picked up a piece of pizza. "Wow, that's hot," he cried, and let it drop to the floor.

"Pick it up," Tim said, standing behind him.

Doug shrugged. "I don't want it. You pick it up."

"You dropped it, come on, pick it up." Tim was furious.

Doug turned around and the two boys glared at each other.

Then Doug grinned. "Sure, I'll pick it up." He stooped down, picked up the slice of pizza, and threw it at Tim. Tim ducked and it missed him but landed against the wall, its cheese and tomato sauce oozing unpleasantly down the flowered wallpaper.

"Oh, my sister will have a fit." Becky ran into the kitchen for some paper towels. When she came back, Doug and his two friends were tossing pieces of pizza to each other, most of it getting on the furniture, the rug, and the walls.

"Stop it, stop it," Becky yelled. She looked to Tim and her friends, who were trying to keep the three from getting at the food. Becky and Lisa took what was left of the pizza into the kitchen, but by that time the place was a mess. The three were throwing beer cans around wildly, saying it was a great game, while the others were frantically trying to stop them.

And then the phone rang. Stacey, who had stood in the background wide-eyed, answered it and called to Becky. "It's Mrs. Marsh. She says there's too much noise; and if there's trouble, she'll call the police. She wants to know what's going on."

"Tell her everything's all right," Becky called back. "And please not to call the police. That's the last thing we need."

As Becky expected, the worst that could happen,

did—Nancy and David came home in the middle of the rumpus. It didn't take long for Nancy to take Stacey up to bed and for David, in his best lawyer's authoritive way, to order everyone out. Becky stood by silently. "Do you want me to stay?" Tim whispered to her.

She gave him a weak smile. "No, you'd better go. And you too, Lisa. I'll call you tomorrow."

When Nancy came back downstairs her face was stony. Becky and David picked up the paper plates and beer cans while Nancy stood by, obviously too angry to even speak. Becky had never seen her sister this way. She seemed frozen with rage, unable to express it short of doing physical violence. She stood with her face tight, her arms folded across her chest, looking as if she had to use all her will to restrain herself from exploding. David threw concerned glances at her, but he kept discreetly silent.

When the worst of the mess had been picked up, Becky couldn't stand it any longer. She faced Nancy. "All right, say it. Bawl me out, don't just stand there like a mummy."

If she expected an explosion, she was disappointed. Nancy returned her defiant eyes coldly. "I'm tired of bawling you out. You're incapable of listening. Let me just say that never again, but never, will you invite anyone over to this house. I say never and I mean it—not for your sixteenth birthday, not for Christmas, not for any excuse you can think of. Just remember that."

The two girls faced each other like two ancient enemies about to enter into a duel. David moved over to Nancy's side and put his arm around her shoulder. "Take it easy, honey. We'll get it cleaned up. It's a mess, but at least no furniture was broken."

Nancy's eyes flared. "Are you going to take her side? Are you saying this is all right?"

"No, but I don't want you to get so upset. It's not worth it. . . ."

Becky found her own voice. "You cannot tell me if I can invite people here or not. This is my house as much as yours," she yelled. "I can invite anyone I darn please and you cannot stop me. You're . . ."—she was searching for the right words—"you're like an old lady. My God, you're not even nineteen, and you act like you were never young, like you never had any fun; you act like a mean old witch. Living with you is like living in, I don't know what, a reformatory. . . ." She turned and pushed her fist hard into the overflowing pail of garbage to make room for more.

"You're right," Nancy yelled back. "I'm not young. I've aged a hundred years this year. I'm not having a chance to be young anymore, taking care of you, worrying about you, taking care of the house, the money, Stacey. Yes, I'm turning into an old woman before my time. . . ."

Becky stared at her sister, at her wild eyes, her beautiful long hair, her slim waist and long legs. "What's happened this year isn't my fault. You're the one who insists on taking the responsibility, saying that you're older. You don't need to take care of me. Listen, I know it's hard on you, but you make it harder. You didn't even want me to take a job and take some pressure off of you. If only . . . "

"If only what?" Nancy asked coldly. "I suppose to-night's an example of your taking care of yourself?"

"No, of course not. It's awful. I feel terrible about it, although it wasn't my fault." Becky turned away. She couldn't say the words that were welling up in her head—"If only you gave me some love. You do everything because you think it's your duty, but you're not like Dad or Mom; you don't give me the tiniest bit of affection. I know it's hard on you, but God, how I miss having some love. . . ."—she wasn't able to say any of it.

Becky watched as Nancy turned and walked out to the back porch with David. That's probably the only clean spot downstairs, she thought. There were bitter tears in her eyes. She felt alone, isolated. The party had been awful, and for a few minutes she felt as if she didn't even have any friends. Then she thought of Tim and Lisa—they and the others had tried to stop the rowdyism. She was just as angry as Nancy about what had happened, so why had they argued about it? Why couldn't they have just agreed that it was terrible and let it go at that? Why couldn't Nancy have been sympathetic about the party's being ruined instead of blaming her? It was her sister's holy righteousness that drove her wild, her jumping in so quickly to blame Becky without even finding out what happened.

Becky knew that somehow or other she had to get out of the house. If she had had any doubts before, that evening's fiasco dispelled them.

Becky spent most of Sunday over at Lisa's house because she didn't want to be with her sister. When she went to work on Monday morning she was still in a bad mood.

By now Becky and Mr. Kowalski—Becky called him Mr. K.—had become good friends. He had told her about himself, how he had been married for thirty years and how lonely he was since his wife died a few years before. "My friends tell me to retire," he said, "but what would I do? I thank God every morning that I have this place to come to. I wouldn't know what to do by myself at home."

And Becky had told him about herself, her father's accident, and her mother's illness. "You told me when you first came here you didn't have a mother," Mr. Kowalski had said drily. "You lied to me about your mother, you lied to me about your age. Now you say you won't be sixteen until July. How do I know you're not telling me a whole cockamamy story?" He shook his head sadly, but his eyes were twinkling. "Kids. They think old people know nothing and that they can tell them anything."

"It's not like that at all," Becky protested. "I just wanted so much to get the job. I thought I was close enough to sixteen. . . ."

"Why you wanted this job so much I don't know. A smart girl like you. . . ."

Becky laughed. "Because I wasn't sixteen. There aren't many jobs for a kid."

"That's what I mean," he said with a wry smile. "You took me for a sucker."

"No," she said sweetly, "just a beautiful person."

"Don't butter me up. I can't afford to raise your salary."

On that hot Monday afternoon when things were still slow, Becky confided some of her anxieties and feelings to Mr. K.

"I've got to get out of that house," she said. "The latest is that my sister doesn't want me to invite my friends over anymore." She told him about the party

106

on Saturday night. "Sure there was a mess, I never denied it was awful. But she acted like I'd committed some crime. You should have seen her. It was scary; even her boyfriend got worried."

"But you say you have no relatives. Except an aunt you don't want to live with. Where is there to go?" Mr. Kowalski gave a sympathetic grunt. "It's hard to be young."

"Oh, boy, you can say that again. The news about my mother is no good; and if she has to stay in the hospital I'm afraid Nancy is going to become my guardian. That would be the pits. Worse yet, if she and David get married, and I'm pretty sure they will, they'll want to adopt Stacey and me. I heard David mention that once. Can you imagine being adopted by your sister who's only three and a half years older but who behaves like sixty?"

"Maybe it wouldn't be so bad. Better than to live with strangers." With the store empty, Mr. K. sat back and lit a cigar.

"You don't understand. It would be awful. I don't want to live with anyone. With things the way they are, I want to be on my own, to be alone."

Mr. Kowalksi looked thoughtful. "I read a story in the paper, in the *New York Times*, that maybe you should look into. It was about young people in Connecticut, more than a hundred of them, I think. They got to be emancipated minors. You have to be sixteen."

"I'll be sixteen in July, the end of next month." She looked at him suspiciously. "What's an emancipated minor? Sounds like some kind of suffragette. Some movement for kids to get the vote?"

Mr. Kowalski laughed. "No, but maybe that's not such a bad idea. Let the kids vote and the old men go

107

to war, instead of the other way around. No, it means a boy or a girl can have all the privileges of an adult before he or she gets to be eighteen. It's a special privilege you get through the court from a judge. You should look into it. The story I read was about kids who couldn't get along at home, and they and their parents agreed to get divorced, so to speak. In a lot of cases it was the parents' idea—they just couldn't cope anymore."

"That's what Nancy keeps saying. But I don't know how she would go for that. . . ."

"She's not your parent. I don't know how much she'd have to say. I guess your mother would have to agree, but I don't know all the details. You should speak to a lawyer." Mr. Kowalski puffed on his cigar contentedly. "It's good to sit down for a while. I'm glad you're here; I need someone young around."

Becky was glad too. Kate, the girl who had been working there, had moved away, and Mr. Kowalski hadn't replaced her. Although this meant more work for Becky, she didn't mind. She felt drawn to the older man, as if he were a surrogate grandfather.

Emancipated minor. The words kept going around in her head for the rest of the day. If she got to be such a thing, Nancy couldn't complain anymore about being responsible for her. She and Nancy would be on an equal footing. But then the thought of her mother dimmed her hopes. She didn't want to do anything to hurt her. She also wondered if she was in a condition to deal with anything legal. Becky wasn't like the kids Mr. K. had read about, kids who couldn't get along with their parents. She didn't have any parents to get along with, so in a way this new provision in the law seemed ideal for her. But it was something she would have to do before Nancy became her guardian or tried to adopt her. Suddenly Becky felt nervously pressed for time, as if she had to get hold of the reins of a runaway horse before it was too late. The whole idea made her feel giddy with excitement and anxious at the same time.

Becky didn't know any lawyer except David, and she felt very unsure about discussing Mr. Kowalski's suggestion with him. He was too close to Nancy, and Becky felt that even though Nancy might not have any legal standing over her, she would have plenty to say. And what she said would not agree with Becky's ideas. She swung back and forth between feeling elated by the thought of being free and independent and becoming despondent because she didn't know where to start.

Becky confided in Tim. It was Sunday afternoon. Tim had tied his canoe on top of his car, and they had driven to the nearby river. It was a soft, warm day with just enough sun filtering through a cloudy sky to be pleasant. With Tim paddling only enough to steer clear of the rocks in the water, the boat drifted with the current. Becky lay back lazily. "This is heaven," she said, looking into Tim's brooding eyes and admiring his healthy, outdoor looks. "We could be in another world miles from anywhere." It was indeed an idyllic spot: for a long stretch the river cut through heavy woods on each side, and only a few other canoes were in sight. There was a rare stillness in the air. "It's hard to remember that life can be so complicated," Becky mused.

"It doesn't have to be," Tim said. "I think you like drama."

"It would be boring without it. I like tragic stories with happy endings. Like my sister Nancy's. She's had a miserable year, we all have, but she's probably going to have a happy ending."

"Are you jealous?"

Becky was about to quickly deny that she was but then thought better of it. "Maybe I am, a little. Not jealous that she's having it, but that I'm not. But maybe I can, maybe I can make something positive out of all this mess, out of my own anger that my family had to get such a lousy break."

"How do you plan to do that?" Tim asked skeptically.

"I have an idea. At least Mr. Kowalski gave me an idea." She told him about being an emancipated minor.

Tim was visibly impressed. "Are you going to do it? It sounds terrific. As if it was made to order for you."

"I know. That's how I feel about it. It's weird—the law seems so far away, as if it has nothing to do with people; and then something like this pops up, and you realize somewhere someone had to have thought of it. I wonder if whoever dreamed this up had kids."

They drifted along for a few minutes before Tim spoke. "So, what are you going to do about it?"

"That's the problem. Do you think I should ask David about it?"

Tim gave that some thought. "I don't know why not," he said finally. "From what you've said he seems like a decent guy. He could at least give you the factual information and tell you what to do—I should think that would be his job as a lawyer and a friend."

"Even if Nancy doesn't like it?"

"Listen, the worst that can happen is that he'd say he didn't want to talk to you about it. You have nothing to lose by asking. Otherwise you're going to just think about it and do nothing, like a dope."

Becky smiled contentedly. "I knew I could count on you to say the right thing. Okay, Timothy," she said affectionately, "watch me go. Becky Jones, Emancipated Minor." She giggled. "Sounds like one of those religious sects. I wish it had a better name."

"You don't need a title. Just plain Becky Jones, a girl to remember." He made it sound important, but Becky as usual masked her feelings with a flip reply.

"Yeah. When you go off to your cooking school you'll forget about me."

"Never, never." Tim's eyes remained serious. "When you have your own pad, will you invite me for the weekend?"

Becky laughed. "You back on that subject again?"

"A fellow can have hopes, can't he?" Tim looked at her with an affectionate grin.

"Is that all you think about?"

"You know better than that," Tim said. "Even if you don't invite me for a weekend, do it, Becky. Don't give up easily."

Becky smiled. "My sister calls me stubborn and pig-headed."

"It's all in the eyes of the beholder," Tim said.

When Becky got home that evening David was at the house. She was eager to ask him if he knew about emancipated minors, but she didn't want to discuss it in front of Nancy. Besides, he had his own news to tell. "We are having a preliminary meeting on Tuesday

111

with the lawyers from the insurance company and the factory," David told her. "I imagine they may be ready to make an offer. But wait," he added quickly, seeing the excited look on Becky's face, "that's just the beginning. Then the bargaining begins. We're not going to accept their first offer, believe me. We're going to have some fun first and get them to where we want them."

"Will that take long?" They couldn't know how anxious she was, Becky thought.

"Who knows? We've got plenty of time. The point is to end up with a settlement that will provide comfortably for you girls and your mother. If we get what we want, I don't care if it takes a year."

"A year?" Becky asked desolately. "It can't take a *year.*"

"Why are you in such a hurry?" Nancy asked. "Whatever we get, it's not going to change our lives that much. It's not money we're going to go out and spend. We'll have to invest it and just use the income. Even if we do get a lot of money, you wouldn't get yours until you're eighteen or twenty-one, or maybe even twenty-five, depending on how your guardian or the court sets it up. Remember, you're still a minor."

"Don't I know it," Becky said, then kept her mouth tightly closed for fear she'd blurt out something she wasn't ready to talk about.

"We could buy me a bike, couldn't we?" Stacey asked. "I mean if we're very rich."

"We will definitely buy you a bike," Becky said before Nancy had a chance to answer. "Are we all coming to this meeting?" she asked David.

"That's not necessary. Nancy of course will be there since she's the one who will have to sign the agreement when we have one. Until your mother gets well your

112

sister has to act as head of the family, and she does have power of attorney." David stroked his beard absently, his eyes on Nancy.

"I don't know why Nancy has to do everything," Stacey said. "She acts like she's our mother."

"I guess she has to," David said kindly. "She's a pretty good substitute, isn't she?" He looked from Stacey to Becky.

Becky remained silent, glad that for a change Stacey was voicing her thoughts about Nancy. "I don't want a substitute," Stacey said flatly.

Becky caught the hurt look on Nancy's face. "Oh, well, Nancy can mess around with lawyers better than we can," she said to Stacey, and then clapped her hand over her mouth when she realized what she had said and saw the flush on David's face. But he laughed good-naturedly and pulled a horrified Nancy over to him. "That's all right, I'm glad someone in this family likes lawyers."

"We like you because you don't seem like a lawyer when you're not in your office," Stacey said innocently.

All evening Becky kept hoping she'd have a minute alone with David. She saw her chance and grabbed it when Nancy went up to her room before she and David left for the evening. "Can I come see you in your office Wednesday afternoon?"

If David was surprised, he didn't show it. "I think it will be all right, but you'd better call the office tomorrow and set up a time with my secretary. Okay?"

"Yes, I will. And David, please don't say anything to Nancy, will you?"

He smiled. "I protect all my clients' confidentiality."

Becky gave him a quick, grateful hug.

10

Monday and Tuesday were long days for Becky. The weather had turned hot; and in spite of Mr. Kowalski's air conditioner, the shop was warm and sticky. She had talked to Lisa on the phone during a slow time Tuesday morning, and Lisa had said she was going swimming with their friends. Becky now wondered if she was crazy to be doing this. No one was forcing her to work; she too could be having a carefree summer, swimming, hiking, going on picnics and traveling to Hartford or New Haven for rock concerts. Even now she could quit the job and have the rest of the summer to herself.

Becky poured herself a cup of coffee, a little coffee and a lot of milk, and sat down on a stool behind the counter.

"Want a doughnut?" Mr. Kowalski asked. "Good and fresh."

"No, thanks, I'm not hungry."

"What's the matter?"

"Nothing," she said. She put down her cup and looked at the old man's gray face. "Do you really think

114

I could be an emancipated minor? Maybe Nancy won't let me."

"I don't think she can stop you. You want a character reference, I'll give it to you. So far you come to work on time, you work hard, you're a good girl."

"Thank you, thank you very much. You're a good boss."

He smiled. "I hope I'm a friend too. An old man, but a friend."

"You are, you certainly are. One of my best friends."

She felt reassured. She had a goal—she was going to establish herself. Maybe when they got the money she'd have enough so she wouldn't have to work all the time. No matter what, though, she'd be free and on her own. There'd be lots of summers for swimming, for fun. . . .

"I've changed my mind," Becky said. "I will have a doughnut. Thanks." She gave him a big smile when he handed one to her.

Tuesday evening Stacey and Becky were waiting on the porch for Nancy to come home from David's office. "Do you think she'll know how much money we're getting?" Stacey asked.

"I don't think so. Remember, David said this was just the beginning, a preliminary meeting. But I wish she'd hurry up."

"Maybe they went out for dinner," Stacey said.

"Oh, God, I hope not. No, she'd call if she was going to do that. Here she comes, here she comes. . . ." They both ran to Nancy when she turned into their driveway.

"Are we going to celebrate?" Becky asked, examining Nancy's face for a clue.

"Not exactly. Wait till we get inside, I'll tell you all there is to tell."

There wasn't much. "They had two lawyers, not bad guys," Nancy said after she had washed her face and stretched out on the porch lounge. "Everyone kind of talked around the bush for a while. They asked me some questions: what I knew about the accident, Dad's condition in the hospital, how Mom was, exactly what has happened since the accident, and what we're living on. I think the insurance man is going to come out here to take a look at the house and at us. They dropped a figure of fifty thousand dollars and David laughed at them."

"Fifty thousand dollars! Isn't that a lot of money?" Stacey asked.

"Not for a man's life," Becky said. "What does David think we can get?"

"You keep asking that. I don't think he knows. He's asking for half a million, that's five hundred thousand dollars, but we'll never get that much. And don't forget, the law firm gets part of it."

"Wow," Stacey said, "we'll be rich."

Becky didn't say anything, but her mind was whirling. She felt so confused. She wanted the money, yet at the same time she hated the idea that anyone—lawyers, insurance men, people who dealt in money—could think they were compensating them for the loss of their father and right now for their mother too. The whole thing was repulsive to her and she didn't know what to do with her feelings. It would be stupid to say she didn't want the money when she did, and yet to be given money to make up for someone's death seemed so crude. "There isn't enough money in the world," she said, "to make up for what happened."

Nancy looked up at her with miserable eyes. "I know," she said grimly. "You two should have been there. I said they weren't bad guys and they weren't, but I hated them. I hated every minute of it. David is going to have to do the bargaining. I don't want any part of it."

Becky went over to the porch steps and sat down, feeling closer to Nancy than she had in a long time. After a few minutes she stood up again and said, "For heaven's sake, let's not sit around here being mournful. Let's go out and get a pizza."

"Yes, let's." Stacey gave a whoop of joy.

"Okay. I don't feel like cooking anyway." Nancy pulled herself up, but her eyes were still unhappy. Becky wanted to make a gesture of affection to let her sister know how much she shared her feeling of distaste for the bargaining, yet she made no move. Slowly she followed Nancy and Stacey to the car thinking how strange it was to feel close and far apart at the same time—she and Nancy were like two runners in a marathon, each preoccupied with her own pacing and goal yet bound together in the same race.

On Wednesday afternoon Becky left the coffee shop early and went to David's office. She hitched a ride with a customer from the shop. After she was ushered in, it took her a few minutes to adjust to David the lawyer, different from the David she knew at home.

"Sit down." David pulled a chair for her close to his desk.

"You're so different here, almost like a stranger." Becky sat down and wondered how to begin what she had to say.

"You want me to take my tie off?" David pulled at

his shirt collar with a grin. "Would that make you feel more comfortable?"

"It probably would, but don't bother. I came to talk business, anyway."

"Good. What's on your mind?"

"Have you ever heard of an emancipated minor?"

"Yes, I have." David looked at her thoughtfully. "Is that something you are considering?"

Becky nodded. "Yes. I'll be sixteen next month." She leaned toward him eagerly. "It sounds as if it's just made for me. I don't know what's going to happen with my mother—Nancy doesn't think she's going to come home. I don't want to say anything against my sister, but I don't want to live with her. Don't you think it would be perfect?"

David leaned back in his big chair. "Did you come to me for personal advice, or to find out about the law?"

"Both, I guess." Becky sat back too, relieved to have gotten the main problem off her chest.

"Well, I don't know that I can give you any advice, or that I want to. This is something very much within your family, and you have to understand I am a bit partisan. But I can tell you about the law. First of all, you can't do anything until you're sixteen. Then you can petition the court, the superior court for juvenile matters, with the facts in the case. Your parent or guardian can also petition the court. Then you will be served with a summons to appear in court at a given date." He gave Becky an amused smile. "A sheriff will come to the house and tap you on the shoulder."

Becky laughed. "The way they do in the movies?"

"Exactly, if the movie is accurate. After that the court may appoint a probation officer or someone from the youth services to investigate what you have said in the petition and report back to the court. Also, since you do not have a guardian yet and your mother may not be able to appear, the court can appoint a lawyer to serve as your guardian. If the court thinks it is necessary, it can also appoint a lawyer to represent your mother. Her rights as a parent have to be protected too."

"It sounds awfully complicated." Becky looked troubled.

"It isn't really. It's just that everyone involved has to be fairly represented. It's similar to a divorce, with each party being given the chance to have his or her say. The court has to determine if the child–parent relationship has irretrievably broken down before declaring that a minor is emancipated."

"But what if my parent can't act as a parent? Then what?"

"The court will have to consider that. Nancy might be subpoenaed to appear. I think in this case she probably would be."

"She'd argue against it," Becky said dismally.

"She might very well. That's the chance you have to take. The judge will listen to you both and make his decision."

"What do you think my chances are?"

David laughed. "I'm not betting either way."

"I don't suppose you'd represent me, would you?" Becky looked at him hopefully.

David shook his head. "No, I couldn't do that. But I'll tell you one thing. I won't represent Nancy either—that is, if you decide to go ahead. I'd want to keep out of it."

"But how would I petition the court?"

David thought about that for a few seconds. "I suppose I could do that for you. I'd want to tell Nancy first. But I could put in the petition and then withdraw from the case and let the court appoint counsel for you. But you'd better know what you're getting into. I'll send you a copy of the state statute so you'll know what it means to be an emancipated minor. It's not all roses; it's taking on responsibility. Think about it carefully, Becky."

She promised that she would; but she knew that she had pretty much made up her mind.

"Are you going to discuss this with Nancy?" David asked, as she got up to leave.

"I'd like to do it when you're there. I think we'd be less likely to get into a big fight." She stood facing him and felt that no matter what happened she had a friend.

David laughed. "Don't count on me to speak for you. But if my being there would help keep you two from getting emotional, I'm willing. You two sisters are something. You know, I believe you really do love each other in spite of everything."

"Of course we do. But that doesn't mean we should live together, does it?" She said good-bye and gave him a kiss on the cheek.

Becky waited impatiently for an opportunity to talk with Nancy, but David was busy working on a brief and didn't come to the house until the weekend. In the meantime, however, he did remember to send her a copy of the Connecticut statute covering the privileges of an emancipated minor. She read the piece of paper over and over again:

120

Sec. 5. An order that a minor is emancipated shall have the following effects: (a) The minor may consent to medical, dental, or psychiatric care, without parental consent, knowledge or liability; (b) the minor may enter into a binding contract; (c) the minor may sue and be sued in his own name; (d) the minor shall be entitled to his own earnings and shall be free of control by his parents or guardian; (e) the minor may establish his own residence; (f) the minor may buy and sell real and personal property; (g) the minor may not thereafter be the subject of a petition under section 46b-120 of the general statutes as an abused, dependent, neglected or uncared for child or youth; (h) the minor may enroll in any school or college, without parental consent; (i) the minor shall be deemed to be over eighteen years of age for purposes of securing an operator's license under subsection (a) of section 14-36 of the general statutes without parental consent; (j) the parents of the minor shall no longer be the guardians of the minor under section 45-53 of the general statutes; (k) the parents of the minor shall be relieved of any obligations respecting his school attendance under section 10-184 of the general statutes; (l) the parents shall be relieved of all obligation to support the minor; (m) the minor shall be emancipated for the purposes of parental liability for his acts under section 52-572 of the general statutes; and (n) the minor may execute releases in his own name under section 14-118 of the general statutes.

121

Sec. 6. Nothing in this act shall affect the status of minors who are or may become emancipated under the common law of this state.

Approved June 14, 1979.

After she received the document in the mail, Becky stopped on her way home from work to see Tim at the store. He took a coffee break, and they sat outside in back of the store drinking sodas. Becky told him about seeing David and showed him the paper. Tim read it over twice before handing it back to her with a low whistle. "It sounds a little scary, doesn't it?"

Becky squinted her eyes against the late afternoon sun and shook her head. "I don't think so. It's what I want."

"But it's being really cut off from your family. I mean, if you get into trouble or anything, there's no one to bail you out." Tim looked worried. "You'd better think about it, kid."

"That's what David said, and I have. But I'm not losing anything—there's no one to bail me out anyway. If I ever did need help, Nancy's helping me wouldn't depend on whether she's legally responsible or not. She either would or she wouldn't, depending on how she felt about it. She's a stickler in a lot of things, but I think if she wanted to do anything for me she would without needing the law to tell her to. Anyway, I don't intend to get into trouble."

"Well, you've got guts." Tim gave her an admiring glance. "Remember what I said—Becky Jones, a girl to remember. Have a lot of other kids done this?"

"Not an awful lot. Mr. Kowalski told me that the article he read said a lot of times the parents want it and

122

petition the court. They don't want the responsibility anymore."

"With parents like that I guess the kids are better off without them," Tim said philosophically.

"Or the kids get into too much trouble," Becky added.

It wasn't until the following Sunday afternoon when Stacey had gone swimming with her friends and Becky was sitting on the porch with Nancy and David that she was able to tell her sister what she wanted to do. The porch was strewn with the Sunday papers. Nancy was on the lounge and David was stretched out on a deck chair, thumbing through the magazine section. Becky was sitting on a swing that their father had made a long time before. Her legs and feet were bare, and with her toes she kept the swing in a gentle, rocking motion.

"Did David tell you that I went to see him?" Becky broke into the lazy afternoon silence.

Nancy raised her head and crooked her arm to give it a place to rest. Her big eyes were alert. "No, he didn't say a word. David?" She looked to him for an answer.

David put down the newspaper. "I was waiting for Becky to tell you." Nancy's expression showed surprise and a trace of hurt. "It's really something that has to be handled between you two. I want to stay out of it as much as possible," he explained.

Picking her words carefully, Becky told her sister about wanting to become an emancipated minor; and with a little help from David she explained what it involved and what it would mean if she became one.

When she was finished talking she handed Nancy the paper stating what she would be able to do. Nancy read it silently and handed it back.

"When I turn sixteen, David said he would petition the court for me," Becky said.

"I thought you wanted to stay out of it," Nancy said to David. She was sitting up now, dangling her bare legs in front of her; with her long hair pinned up against the heat, she looked cool and pretty.

"I won't do it if you'd rather I didn't. But who petitions the court doesn't make much difference. I would withdraw and let the court appoint counsel."

"I guess it doesn't matter," Nancy said indifferently. "But the whole idea . . . it comes as quite a surprise. I didn't know you were so miserable here." She turned to Becky accusingly. "I don't know what you have to complain about. . . . "

"I'm not complaining. I just want to be on my own. Can't you understand that?"

"Frankly, no. If you want to know the truth, I don't think you're capable of being on your own."

Becky pushed the swing harder. "I'd expect you to say that. That's the heart of the trouble, what you think I'm capable of and what I actually do. I suppose for me to be working all summer doesn't mean a thing to you."

"Oh, that job. You talk about it as if it were some wonderful accomplishment. No, I don't especially think it's anything to be so proud of."

"I don't know why I talk about anything with you," Becky said, unable to keep her voice from becoming shrill. "You put down everything I do. I don't care what you say. I'm going to go ahead and try to get out

124

of this trap, to be free. And if you were any kind of a decent sister, you wouldn't stand in my way."

"I'll have to do what I think best," Nancy said relatively calmly. She looked to David. "If she does go through with this and succeeds, what happens if and when we get the settlement? I mean, what if she is an emancipated minor before we get an agreement?"

"I guess she'd have the same rights you'd have. She'd have to agree to the arrangement and she'd also be able to ask for her share. She'd have the rights of an adult." David glanced at Becky and gave a frustrated smile. "I hope it won't complicate things."

"You don't have to worry," Becky said. "I'm not going to fight about money. I'll leave that up to you two."

"You know how I feel about that. The whole settlement is David's department. He can do all the fighting."

David grinned. "Great clients, both of you. But you're right, that's what you have a lawyer for." He looked at Nancy. "Come on, I'll take you downtown and buy you some ice cream." He pulled Nancy up from the lounge.

Becky watched them go to David's car. "Bring me back some maple walnut," she called after them. She continued to swing, relieved to have gone through the hurdle of telling Nancy her plans. It could have been worse, she thought, although what Nancy would or could do to interfere remained to be seen. But Nancy had not shaken her desire to carry out her plan.

Ever since she had gotten the legal document and been reading and rereading it, there had been moments when she was tempted to tear it up and throw it away. At one point she had even gone so far as to bury it under a pile of underwear in her bureau drawer because it was scary to think about. It sounded so final: once she was on her own there would be no turning back. It was worse than getting married, she thought. Then, if you had to, you could get a divorce; but you couldn't divorce yourself.

She went through lightning changes of feelings about it: one minute thinking that coming home from work to an empty place with no one, not even little Stacey, to talk to, would be unbearable; and the next, envisioning her own place, eating when she felt like it, doing what she felt like, as divine. Tim's saying she had guts had made her feel good, and even Nancy's predictable put-down strengthened her resolve.

When she had taken the piece of paper out of the drawer and read it again for the nth time, the possibilities had seemed endless. She had no intention of working in a little coffee shop forever; there was a big world out there, and in her best moments she saw herself as a woman with a successful business career. These were the times when she studied her father's picture and could hear him saying, "You can do it, Becky, you can make what you want of yourself."

Becky went on swinging, thinking not about Nancy but about what the future might hold. At least she was taking action, making a change that might have its risks but that would open up her life to a new and exciting experience.

11

Waiting. Becky felt as if she spent half her life waiting for something. Now it was for her sixteenth birthday. She kept wondering if she would hear from her mother for her birthday. If she didn't, she was going to ask the doctor to let her go see Mrs. Jones. As she said to Lisa, "Sixteen is an important one."

"Are you going to have a party?" Lisa asked.

"I don't know." She couldn't tell even her closest friend what Nancy had said about not having anymore friends over. It made her feel so childish.

About a week before her birthday, she asked Nancy at breakfast if she had really meant what she said about not inviting anyone to the house.

"I meant it when I said it," Nancy replied. "I'm not a monster, you know; but there are so many decisions, so many things on my mind." She poured coffee for herself and Becky. Stacey was still upstairs sleeping. "David asked me to marry him." The announcement didn't come as any big surprise to Becky.

"But that's wonderful," Becky said excitedly. She

was about to throw her arms around Nancy but was stopped by her sister's woebegone face. "What's the matter?"

"I don't know what to do. I adore David, but he's ten years older than I am; and I don't know . . . I feel that I'm too young, I'm not ready. I haven't had a chance. Even before the accident, you don't know, Mom depended on me so much. She wasn't well, and she wanted me to help her decide things. Everything, from what to have for Sunday dinner to whether to tell Dad she'd bought a new dress. As if he'd care." Nancy spoke as if she'd suddenly, without planning it, had to let out thoughts she'd been carrying around with her for years. "One Christmas he wanted to buy her a fur coat, but she wouldn't take it; and then she cried about it to me after, worrying that she'd hurt his feelings. I don't feel that I was ever young. None of it was your fault, Becky; it's just that I was the oldest and she leaned on me. You had Dad, anyway."

"I'm sorry . . . I never knew. I've just been thinking all along that you're uptight. I didn't know you had so much to worry about."

"I *am* uptight. That's the trouble. David's good for me, he's so easygoing. I hope he can put up with me. I admire you because you're strong and you'll fight for what you want. I'm accepting, and I worry." Nancy studied her coffee cup. "This is a heck of a time to get into a discussion like this," she said, glancing at the clock on the wall. "We've both got to get to work."

"But we're in it, and it's important," Becky said. "No one will kill us if we're a few minutes late. We never are."

Nancy laughed. "See, that's what I mean. You're not afraid to do what you want, and I am."

"Do you want to marry David? That's the important thing." Becky looked directly into her sister's eyes.

"I love him, I know that. I guess I just have the jitters making such an important decision. I know I don't want to lose him."

"I don't honestly understand what you're afraid of if you do love him. Getting married doesn't have to mean being settled. You don't have to have kids right away. The two of you will have fun—you can go on trips together, you can do a lot of things. David can make waves. . . . I think if you let go more he would, too. But you'd be safe with him."

"Is that a reason to get married, to be safe? Sounds funny coming from you." Nancy had a whimsical smile.

"I mean, safe to let yourself go. He'll help you relax more. As you said, he's good for you. I think you're good for each other."

Nancy laughed. "I hope so. I really have to go." She got up from the table; her eyes were teary. "We haven't really talked this way before, have we. And at a hurried breakfast, of all things."

"That's the way it happens. I'm glad. And what about my birthday? Can I ask some kids over?"

"We'll talk about it tonight. I really have to go now." She went out, and Becky followed her soon after.

When Becky came home from work, Nancy was in the kitchen mixing a wine marinade for a chicken. She was humming, and her face was flushed. There was an air of excitement about her.

"What's going on?" Becky asked.

"Nothing, really." She looked up at Becky with a

telltale smile. "I took your advice. Sooner than I expected."

"What advice?"

"You know, what you said this morning. That I should let myself go."

"What are you going to do?" Becky's voice was a little alarmed.

"Nothing serious. And don't laugh at me. David's been asking me to go to the horse races with him, and I kept saying no. We're going on Saturday. I'm really excited about it. I've never been to anything like that."

Becky laughed, somewhat relieved. "Is that all? I thought you were about to tell me you were going to elope, or fly to Europe, do something terribly wild."

"Well, you'll have to admit that for me to go to the races is something new," Nancy said primly.

"You'll have to have a big hat." Becky picked up a stalk of celery from the assorted vegetables Nancy was washing and nibbled on it.

"Why do I need a big hat?"

"That's what ladies wear to the races. Will you bet?"

"Yes, of course. But only two dollars on a horse. I'm not going completely wild." She put the chicken and the vegetables in a pot and put the pot on the stove. Nancy glanced at the clock. "David's coming to dinner; he should be here soon."

"You can't make a lot of money betting only two dollars," Becky commented.

Stacey came into the kitchen and wanted to know what they were talking about. Becky told her. "Can I come?" she asked Nancy. "I love horses. I may want to ride in races when I grow up."

"I don't know if it's a place for a little girl," Nancy said. "I'll have to ask David."

"She'd probably have the time of her life," Becky said.

David was in the house only a few minutes when, against Nancy's admonishment to let him sit down and have a beer, Stacey asked David if she could go with them on Saturday. "I don't know why not," he said, glancing at Nancy. "If your sister doesn't mind."

"Do children go to the racetrack?"

David laughed. "I've seen babies there in strollers and old men and women who could hardly walk. It's for all ages, darling." He opened the can of beer Nancy gave him and sat down. "How about you, Becky—you want to come? We can make it a family party."

"You'll corrupt the whole family," Nancy said.

"Good, I want to be corrupted. Sure, I'd love to go."

"This could be your birthday celebration," Nancy suggested. "Instead of having a party?" She looked at Becky questioningly.

"That would be nice."

Saturday was a lovely summer day. A storm the night before had cleared the humidity away, and in the morning the air was fresh and clean. Becky came down to breakfast without really expecting any presents, since the trip to the racetrack would be more than enough for her, but there were packages at her place. Stacey had made her a beaded bracelet; there were books from Nancy; and Aunt Marie had sent a card with five dollars in it. No word from her mother. "Not even a card," Becky commented to Nancy sadly.

"Maybe she couldn't find one," Stacey said. "Or maybe she just forgot."

"I guess she forgot," Becky said dismally, knowing that she would never get over the fact that their mother was in a mental institution. If she had been physically ill, at least they would be able to communicate, Becky thought. And at the same time it was this cutoff feeling, the sense of having lost an anchor, weak as it was, that made her push to be on her own. Now that she was sixteen, Becky planned to go to see David at his office as soon as possible.

In the meantime Nancy and Stacey were singing "Happy Birthday." At nine o'clock David came to pick them up. He gave her some records.

Becky kept a tight hold on Stacey's hand, and her eyes never left Nancy's red dress. Following Nancy and David through the crowd of people wasn't easy. There was so much to look at, and she could feel, actually breathe in, the tense excitement in the air. Becky had never seen a crowd like this before. There was no one kind of person, as one might see at a football game or a rock concert. Here there was a mixture of everybody: old ladies who looked as if they didn't have a dime, women with tots pulling on their arm, sharp men, elegant couples, long-haired youths, jazzy girls in jeans, old men with sad faces. . . . They were all here for the same reasons: for the thrill of watching the horses run and with the hope that theirs would win. Becky loved it: the colors, the people, the huge betting area with its lines of people at each window, the smell of hot dogs and beer, the gala grandstand, and best of all the track itself, decked out with flags, smooth and inviting.

David led them into the clubhouse where there was a large, comfortable dining room with a wall of glass through which they could get a good view of the track. "Let's get seated and then I'll go and place your bets," he told them.

Becky would have liked to sit outside in the grandstand with the general crowd, but she knew that David was being a generous host. He gave them each a racing form and then handed Becky and Stacey each twenty-five dollars. "This is yours, do what you want. If you lose it all there isn't anymore. If you win you keep the winnings."

Becky was overwhelmed. "How little can I bet?"

"Two dollars," David told her. "But you and Stacey can go in together if you want, with a dollar each."

"How do we know what horse to bet on?" Stacey asked.

David laughed. "You don't. Just guess."

Becky looked up from the news sheet David had also given her. "I'm betting on White Star in the first race. The jockey's name is Tim."

"Then I'll bet on him too," Stacey said.

Nancy studied her racing sheet thoroughly and in her efficient way analyzed the background of each horse before she made her decision.

David came back with their betting tickets just as the horses were led out of the paddock. Becky and Stacey jumped up with excitement. "I wish I was riding one of them." Speechlessly Becky admired her horse, number 4.

"*They're off. . . .*" With one voice the crowd was on its feet, every eye following the horses. Becky watched number 4 start near the lead, then drop behind, then edge up on the inside of the curve. "I think I am going to die of excitement." She was clutching Stacey's arm;

and at the finish, with the roar of the crowd and the clutch of horses crossing the line, she didn't know who had won. David told Becky her horse had come in second.

"Did I win anything?" she asked.

"Not this time. Your money was on first."

When David ordered lunch Becky was too excited to eat. With the third race she was ahead four dollars. By the seventh race she was behind two dollars and determined to win with the eighth and last race.

But before that race started, David came back to their table after placing the bets with a very pretty girl and a man with a curling mustache. He introduced them as friends of his, Honey and Fred. He and Fred had been at law school together. "They live pretty near here and they want us to go back to their place after the races."

"Please come," the girl said. "I can't promise an elegant meal, but I can rustle up something. It would be such fun. Fred was just talking about David the other day, saying he wanted to get in touch with him. And here he is." She had a wide, friendly smile.

"Sounds good to me," Nancy said. "But there are four of us. Won't that be a lot of trouble?"

"No, of course not." Fred and David arranged where to meet, and Honey and Fred left to go back to their own seats.

"There won't be four," Becky said to Nancy. "I'm going home to meet Tim."

"You can't do that." Nancy shook her head to emphasize her no. "How will you get home? You didn't tell me you'd made a date with him."

"I hadn't expected you were going to stay out for

dinner. Anyway, it's my birthday and I want to spend part of it with him. I can get home okay, don't worry. It's no problem."

"Of course it's a problem. You don't know your way around the subways, and they're dangerous. I won't let you do it. You can call Tim from Honey and Fred's house and tell him you'll see him tomorrow." Nancy took a small mirror from her bag and fussed with her hair.

"Look, Nancy, I don't want to have a fight. It's been a beautiful day, but I *am* going home. I'm sixteen now, remember?" She tried to make light of it.

"I don't care how old you are. I am not going to let you take a subway and train home alone from here. Just forget that. You are not emancipated, or whatever you call it, yet." Her face was set in a firm line.

Becky's mouth was equally firm. "I don't think you can stop me," she said quietly. The two girls faced each other, and Becky knew that no matter how many close moments they might have together, no matter how much love there was between them, the struggle between them would never end. My God, she thought, when we're two old ladies we'll still be arguing. But she felt her own strength and determination.

When David came back Becky asked him if he would drop her at the subway station when they left. Nancy told him curtly that Becky was going home. "If you don't want to do it, I'll walk," Becky said, looking at David's perplexed face. She didn't want to be the cause of a fight between the two of them.

Becky didn't even bet on the last race. She sat miserably, feeling Nancy's displeasure and trying to think of how wonderful the day had been up until then.

The short ride to the subway was grim and silent. When Becky was leaving she put her hand on Nancy's for a few seconds. "Have a good time, and don't worry about me." Nancy kept looking out the window and didn't answer.

Becky ran to the token booth rather pleased with herself and excited about being on her own. She was sixteen years old and able to take care of herself. The station was crowded, probably with people from the racetrack, she figured. She went through the crowd to a platform marked for trains to Manhattan. A train came roaring into the station, but Becky couldn't see where it was going, so she let it go by. After she let a second one leave without getting on, she went over to a motherly looking woman and asked her what train to take to Grand Central Station. The woman hugged her pocketbook to her chest, muttered something in a foreign language, and turned away.

Becky made up her mind to get on the next train. As long as she got into Manhattan she could find her way to the station. By this time the crowd was thinning out, and Becky had no trouble finding a seat in the train. She was reading all the ads for the third time when it seemed to her she'd been riding for a long time. She was startled to see that the train was almost empty. There was one old man in a corner, snoring loudly, and two young men across the aisle staring into space. They were paying no attention to her, but she began to think of all the terrible subway stories she'd heard and of Nancy's admonitions. The train was traveling aboveground, and on the spur of the moment, Becky got up and got out at the next station.

The sky had become dark with clouds and the air

chilly. Standing alone on the cold platform, Becky felt foolish and a little nervous. She didn't know why she had gotten off the train, and she was annoyed with her case of nerves. She was determined not to give Nancy a chance to say "I told you so, I knew you wouldn't know how to get home on your own."

She waited twenty-five minutes before another train came. It was almost as empty as the one she'd gotten off, but she sat down near two girls and felt more secure. She didn't think they were too much older than she was and watching them made her feel better. They probably rode the subways all the time, and if they could, she could.

After what seemed another too-long time, the train came to a station marked "42nd Street." Becky got out quickly and went up the stairs to the street. The streets were crowded, and she looked around for any sign of Grand Central Station. The street sign said "Times Square." This time she went up to a policeman and asked him where the station was. "Go down to the subway and take a shuttle across town," he told her.

"Couldn't I walk there?"

He stared at her. "I guess you could, miss. It's kind of a long walk, though."

"Which way do I go?"

He stopped to blow his whistle. "I gotta take care of the traffic, lady. Just keep walking on Forty-second Street and you'll come to it."

Becky decided she'd rather walk miles than go back into the subway. Although it was chilly, the air felt good after the dank subway tunnel. The policeman's directions were hurried, so she wasn't sure she was walking in the right directon. When she passed Avenue of the Americas and got to Fifth Avenue and the public library, she was sure she was headed right. She knew that much about New York. It was a long walk; and not being used to city pavements or walking in heels, her legs began to ache. Becky realized she hadn't eaten since lunch, and it was now after seven o'clock. She went into a Chock full o' Nuts shop and got herself a doughnut and a cup of coffee. She thought longingly of being home and having dinner out with Tim, and wondered if she should call him. Since she didn't know what train she would make, she decided it would be silly.

The coffee made her feel better, and Becky went back to the street with confidence again, pleased that she had gotten this far even though it had taken her much too long. When finally she reached the train station, she thought ruefully that her journey had been as arduous as a safari in Africa.

But it wasn't over yet. When she discovered that she had missed her train by five minutes, she could have killed herself for stopping to eat. There wouldn't be another one for two hours. Furious, she tried reaching Tim on the phone but got no answer. She made up her mind that she'd make him swear not to tell anyone, especially Nancy, how long it had taken her to get home.

Becky went to the ladies' room and washed her face, combed her hair, put on fresh makeup, and sat down to wait. After a short while, she became restless and went into the main part of the station. She bought a magazine and went back to the waiting room to sit down and read. She took off her shoes and put them in her lap with her pocketbook. After reading a few pages, she fell asleep.

She awoke to the sound of a baby crying and sat up with a start, confused about where she was. A young woman sitting next to her smiled apologetically as she rocked her infant. "Sorry she woke you up."

"That's all right." Becky looked at the big clock on the wall and got up hurriedly. She had only a few minutes to make her train. If she missed this one she'd be in the station for the night. As she ran, she realized she should be calling Tim or Nancy, but there wasn't time. She raced through the gate and down the platform, reaching the train just in time. The door closed behind her and the train pulled out. She sank down on a seat, breathless.

It was not a happy journey home. Becky was worried sick. It would be after eleven when she got to the station. There weren't any taxis at that time of night, and Becky dreaded having to call Nancy to come and get her. If Nancy was home. Becky thought she would be by that time, since Stacey would be exhausted after the long day. I've made a mess of it, Becky thought morosely. She could just hear Nancy saying, "I told you you wouldn't know how to get home by yourself."

But she was getting home, that was the important thing. Becky straightened her back resolutely. She wasn't going to let Nancy make her feel like a twerp. So she had made some mistakes. Nancy would too if she was in a city where she didn't know her way around. But she hadn't been afraid to try, and Nancy would have been; that was the difference.

By the time the train pulled into the New Salem station, Becky's mood of despair had left her. Although she was still nervous about facing Nancy and Tim, she wasn't going to let anyone make her feel like an idiot because it had taken her so long to get home. Nothing had happened to her, she had managed, and if she was late she was sorry but it wasn't the end of the world.

The station was cold and dreary, and no one was there. For all her determination, Becky's heart was beating nervously as she dropped a dime into the telephone slot to call home. Nancy's voice answered almost immediately. "Becky," her sister shrieked. "Where are you? We're all worried sick. Are you all right? Where are you?"

"I'm at the station. Have you heard anything from Tim?"

"He's here. He's been going back and forth to the station all night. We've just been debating whether to call the police. Why the devil haven't you called us?" Nancy's anxious voice was turning to anger.

"I'll tell you when I get home. Will Tim come and get me?"

"I guess so. But you come right home. I don't want you going off someplace with him now."

Becky hesitated. She really wanted to stop someplace with Tim and get something to eat, and she didn't like Nancy's tone of voice. But she decided she'd better not. "Don't worry, I'll come home." Suddenly she felt very tired. It was going to be more of the same when she got home. Nancy would yell at her, she'd lose her temper . . . and all for what? Because she had done something on her own that her sister didn't want her to do. Why should she have to account for every move she made and have Nancy order her not to stop with Tim. On her sixteenth birthday too.

Tim was almost as angry as Nancy. "You could have telephoned," he said, after she had explained all that had happened.

"I tried. But there was no answer at your house. Listen, I'm going to get it from Nancy when I get home. Not you too, please. This was supposed to have been a birthday celebration." She sighed deeply.

"I wish we could stop someplace," Tim said.

"So do I. But I can't stand anymore fighting. Nancy'll be bad enough without making it worse."

Becky's fears were fully realized. Nancy was furious. She started yelling as soon as Becky walked into the house. Becky kept a stony silence. She went to the refrigerator, took out some cold roast beef, and made herself a sandwich. With that and a glass of milk in her hands, she said to Nancy, "I'm going upstairs to my room. If you are interested in hearing what happened, I'll tell you tomorrow when you've gotten your screaming out of your system. And," she added in a strong, clear voice, "soon you won't have to worry about where I go or when I come home. I won't be here for you to yell at. That should be a relief to you." With that she marched out of the kitchen and up to her room.

With her door closed behind her, she sat down to eat. But her appetite had faded. She ate only half her sandwich and drank a little of the milk.

Her sixteenth birthday had come and gone. Had it ended in total disaster, she wondered. No, she decided, for as tired and as disappointed as she was, she had a sense of her strength. She missed terribly not having had the evening with Tim, yet she *had* been able to take care of herself in a fashion; and as a result she felt freer from Nancy's hold. And not letting her sister goad her into a big fight must in itself be some sign of improvement.

Becky fell into bed without even washing her face. In minutes she was fast asleep.

141

12

"Okay," David said, "now all you have to do is sign your name."

Becky looked lovingly at the legal form once more. It was her petition to the juvenile court for a hearing. She was sitting in David's office a few days after her birthday. Together they had worded her reasons for wanting to be an emancipated minor: "Because I don't have any parents at home," Becky had said; "my father is dead and my mother is in a mental hospital. I do not want my sister, three and a half years older, to be my guardian or to adopt me. We don't get along. I have a job, I expect some money to be coming to me, and I want to live alone. I can take care of myself financially as well as otherwise."

Becky signed her name in clear, large letters.

"The judge will appoint a lawyer to represent you, and you'll get a summons to appear in court. I wish you luck," David said.

"Is Nancy very mad?'

"She's not happy about it."

"What about you?"

"Don't ask me a dumb question. I love Nancy and I don't like to see her unhappy."

"I'm sorry."

Becky walked out of the office wondering if it would be bad luck to buy the heart-backed wicker chair she had seen and wanted for her own place. Wherever that would be. For a moment she felt the panic again—an apartment of her own. What if she signed a lease and then couldn't pay the rent; could she be put in jail for that? Suddenly she became aware of everything she didn't know. How did Nancy know so much about taking care of things? I wish I'd paid more attention, Becky thought; but I'll learn. On her way to the bus she stopped in front of a butcher shop and studied a paper in the window showing the different cuts of beef. Then she burst into giggles. A woman glanced at her and crossed to the other side of the street, which only made Becky laugh harder.

Becky and her two sisters were in the kitchen eating supper a couple of weeks later when Stacey saw a police car pull into the driveway. She jumped up. "Hey, there's a police car here."

Becky dropped her fork. "I think it's for me," she said weakly.

"For you?" Nancy shrieked. "What have you done now?"

"I haven't done anything. It's a summons."

"A summons is for something. Tell me quick...."

Stacey answered the knock on the door. "Are you Rebecca Jones?" The officer looked Stacey up and down, holding a paper in his hand.

Becky stood up. It took her a few seconds to remember what her real name was. "No, I am.'"

The sheriff tapped her on the shoulder and handed her the paper. "This is for you." Foolishly she said, "Thank you," and then turned away, embarrassed.

The whole thing took less than two minutes. Becky listened to the sheriff drive away. She opened the document and read it twice. "It's a summons to appear in the juvenile court on August twenty-third at nine o'clock in the morning," she told Nancy, and handed it to her. Stacey read it looking over her sister's shoulder, and Nancy gave it back to Becky.

"It looks scary," Stacey said, breaking the silence.

"I don't think so. It looks official. That's what I want." She kept looking at Nancy, but her sister's face was impassive. "Aren't you going to say anything?" Becky burst out.

"I've said all there is to say. I'll save the rest for the twenty-third." Nancy got busy clearing the table.

"Are you going to be there?"

"Yes, I'm going to be there. I guess I'll get one of these too."

"A summons like this?" Becky frowned.

"Yes." Then she looked at Becky with a thin smile. "I have rights too."

When Becky came home from work the next afternoon, Stacey handed her a message to call Mr. Richard Bracioli. "Sounds like something to eat." Becky studied the name Stacey had carefully printed.

"He said to call as soon as you got home," Stacey said.

Becky dialed the number nervously. As she expected, Mr. Bracioli was her court-appointed lawyer,

144

and she made an appointment to see him two days later. Then she phoned Lisa and asked her to come over because she had to talk to someone.

A short while later her friend was sitting on her bed while Becky brought her up to date on her life.

"Where will you live?" Lisa asked.

"I don't know—I'll have to find a place. I guess it will depend on how much money I have."

"Are you going to take your furniture with you?" Both girls looked around the room. There wasn't much—her bed, the makeshift desk, an old bureau, one chair, her books, posters, and a framed picture of her father on the bureau.

"I'll have to ask Nancy," Becky said. "The bed is mine, my mother bought it for me when I was twelve. Nancy has to let me take that." She got up from the chair where she had been sitting and walked around nervously. "Do you think it's really going to happen? That I'll really be on my own?"

Lisa nodded. "Yes, I do. You've gone this far."

"Do you think I'm crazy?"

Lisa seemed to be studying her answer. "No, not for you. I wouldn't want it, but you're different and your whole life is different. You may be lonely, but maybe you won't mind."

"Why should I be lonely?" Becky asked sharply. "I'll still have friends. Heck, I'm not moving someplace far away." She was nervous enough without having Lisa raise problems.

"Don't get mad. You asked me what I thought and I'm telling you. I don't think you should expect it to be a hundred percent terrific. I can think of a lot of things that would bother me."

"Thanks a lot. I thought you'd support me. Please, I don't want to hear about the things that would bother you," Becky said; then a few minutes later she asked, "What are they?" and sat on the edge of her desk.

"Oh, I'd probably worry about money, and being in a place alone, getting broken into . . . what I'd do when I was sick, forgetting things on the stove . . . all kinds of things. But that's me, not you," her friend added hastily.

"Yeah, I know," Becky said glumly, wishing Lisa hadn't voiced some of the things that had already occurred to her. "I hope the lawyer isn't a creep."

"I think what you're doing is fantastic, I really do. I do support you. I just wouldn't have the guts. I think you're someone terribly special, Becky. After all the things that have happened to you, some kids would crack up or not give a damn; but for you to work the way you do and now make yourself independent, I think it's terrific, honestly."

Becky grinned. "Well, thanks for those kind words. Anytime you want my autograph, I'll be glad to oblige."

The lawyer was young, even younger than David, and he wasn't a creep. He had a pleasant, homely face with a nose that was too long, but a generous mouth and a friendly smile. He was in a small office two buildings down from where David worked, and his wife was his secretary. "We're a mom-and-pop business," he said to Becky with a grin as he introduced himself.

He picked up a copy of her petition and asked her to tell him from the beginning about herself and her reasons for wanting to become emancipated. Becky repeated her story for what seemed to her the hundredth time.

"What do you think?" she asked after she finished.

"It sounds reasonable to me. So long as you know what you're getting into. Have you read what the law provides?" Becky nodded. "Then you know what you're taking on. Remember, if you get into trouble there's going to be no one to bail you out. You're going to have to take care of your own money, your own health, your own responsibility as a member of society. No kid stuff anymore."

"I know that."

"David Cimino told me that the court is subpoenaing your older sister. He's going to represent her, I believe."

Becky jumped in the chair. "But he told me he wouldn't. He said he was staying out of it."

"I guess he changed his mind. But I wouldn't worry. I know David well. He's a fair-minded guy, he wouldn't do anything to hurt you."

"But my sister's against this, so he will be too." Becky was furious.

"He can only state her reasons, and actually she doesn't have much standing in court as she isn't your guardian or parent. I think we'll have to send someone down to see your mother. Probably a social worker will go to determine how well she can function. The court may want to appoint a lawyer to represent her too."

"I'd like to try to see her first. She doesn't know anything about this."

"Give me her doctor's name. We'll contact him first. But if you want to see her, go ahead; that's up to you."

147

When Becky left her lawyer's office, it took her about two minutes to decide to march herself up to David's office. During the twenty minutes that she had to wait before she could see him, she worked herself into a towering rage.

"Hello." David greeted her with a warm smile. "This is a pleasant surprise. Sit down."

"I don't want to sit down. You said you were going to keep out of my affairs, and now Mr. Bracioli told me that you're going to represent Nancy. You lied to me. I think it's disgusting."

"Whoa, take it easy. Sit down, relax. I'm sorry you heard about it from Richard. I was going to tell you when I saw you. Nancy and I talked it over and we decided it would be silly for her to run up a legal bill. And you might get someone much tougher than I am, someone very opposed to the idea of kids being on their own. I'll go to court with Nancy, but she'll speak for herself. I probably won't have to say a word. The judge is going to make the decision, no one else. All we can do is present him with the facts in the case. I don't think you have anything to worry about. If the judge thinks you should be allowed to be emancipated, you will be; and if he doesn't, you won't be. It's up to him."

Becky left, still dissatisfied with David's decision to represent Nancy. She stopped to see Tim on her way home, but he was too busy to express more than a few words of understanding about her reaction before turning away to wait on a customer.

Becky walked home slowly, submerging herself in her sense of isolation. When she arrived at her house, she walked up the hill. She hadn't been there since the day she had picked the mushrooms. She stretched out on a patch of bright green moss and closed her eyes. Silly things came to mind: she tried to remember how her parents had gotten her big bed through the narrow door to her room; what her father had given her for her last birthday; and where she had put a small amethyst ring her mother had once given her. Had Lisa ever given her back the book of poems she had borrowed?

She didn't know why she was thinking of these things now. And then she wondered if anyone was ever happy.

"I feel awful asking for more time off," Becky said to Mr. Kowalski the next day, "but I'll have to be in court on the twenty-third."

"I know, you told me," he said patiently. He had followed her events with great interest.

"Golly, I must be losing my mind."

"Maybe you have too much on it. What about your mother, does she know about this?"

"I'm going to see her on Sunday. It makes me nervous."

"Take a doughnut, it's good for your nerves."

Becky laughed. "Especially a jelly doughnut, they're the best."

"Have you thought about where you're going to live? That is, if you become such a big shot, grown-up lady?"

"No, I'll have to find a place."

"Maybe I'll have an apartment."

Becky swallowed her mouthful of doughnut quickly. "You're kidding. You say it so calmly, like it's a nice day today. Have you really got an apartment?" Her voice went up high.

149

"Maybe. Nothing great to write home about. But maybe you'll like it. We'll see when the time comes."

"You won't tell me about it? You can't do this to me. You're my friend. Where is it? You can tell me that."

Mr. Kowalski gave her his half-smile. "Better make more egg sandwiches. Mrs. Fineberg will bring her kids in from swimming and they like egg sandwiches."

"You creep. How many should I make?"

"About half a dozen, that should be enough. And lots of mayonnaise."

13

Becky stared at the sickly green wall of the small waiting room in the hospital and wondered why anyone would have picked such a dismal color. She crossed and uncrossed her legs nervously. The hospital social worker who had spoken with her had said the same thing as the doctor: "You can only spend a short time with your mother, and don't upset her." They made her feel like an outsider, as if her mother belonged to them, not to her.

She stood up when her mother and a nurse appeared in the doorway. Becky stopped for a few seconds before she ran up to put her arms around her. No one had prepared her for the change. The regular reports from the doctor had said that he didn't advise them to visit and that their mother was well taken care of and not unhappy. It had never occurred to Becky that in telling them to stay away, the doctor had been protecting them perhaps more than their mother.

Mrs. Jones had shrunk; she had become an old

woman with wispy hair and a stooped walk. Her face, however, was smooth, almost childlike, as if someone had scrubbed away its natural life signs. The contrast between her mother's face and her body unnerved Becky. She felt as if someone were playing a horrible joke and had given her mother a foolish mask.

Becky felt silly saying "How are you?" but she said it anyway.

"I'm fine," her mother said gaily. "They gave me medicine so I'd have a good cleaning out. The medicine tasted terrible, but the nurse said I had a real good bowel movement." She said it with great pride.

"Come and sit down and have a nice chat with your daughter." The nurse led Mrs. Jones gently to a chair.

Becky sat beside her and held one of her mother's hands in hers. She waited for the nurse to leave, but the young, pale-faced woman took a chair on the opposite side of the room. She picked up a magazine and settled herself comfortably.

"Mom, you look very pretty," Becky said. Her mother's face was beautiful in a strange, lifeless way. Becky remembered reading someplace that that was the way people looked when they were dead, and she shuddered.

"I am not going to sit next to that Ida Kronin in the dining room. She steals all my food. Nasty pig of a woman. Too fat anyway." Her mother took her hand away from Becky and folded her hands in her lap. "Your hand is wet," she said, and then wiped both her hands on her skirt.

"Mom, I have something I'd like to tell you. I'm going to move out of the house, I'm going to get my own apartment. I'm very excited about it."

152

Her mother giggled. "You mustn't get excited." She glanced over at the nurse. "They don't like it here if you get excited." She leaned closer to Becky. "It's very dangerous."

"Mom, darling . . . can you understand what I'm saying? I'm moving out on my own. Someone may come to talk to you about it to get your okay."

"I think that medicine is working again. Nurse, nurse . . . you'd better get me to a bathroom or I'll have an accident again." She began to whimper. "I don't want to have an accident and get spanked. . . ."

The nurse jumped up. "It's all right, Mrs. Jones. Come, we'll get you to a bathroom; but it's probably another false alarm." She glanced at Becky. "We'd better go. I hope you had a nice visit. . . ."

"You don't spank her, do you?" Becky was shocked.

"No, of course not. It's a childhood memory for her." She gave Becky a pat. "Believe me, she is treated very well. We'd better go." Mrs. Jones was tugging at her arm.

Her mother didn't look back to say good-bye.

Becky watched them go out into the corridor, hoping they would get out of the room before she burst into tears. But she didn't cry when they left. She thought she might never cry again. Everything inside of her felt dry; her mouth, her tongue, her whole body felt as if it had been put through an old-fashioned wringer.

Riding home, Becky kept her eyes glued to the window. She was afraid she would cry if she really looked at the families on the bus with her, laden with picnic baskets, plastic bags of wet bathing suits and towels, and tired small children clinging to their parents' hands. Mothers and fathers and children. In a way she was glad that her father didn't have to see her mother the way she was now. But if her father hadn't been killed, her mother might not be that way.... If only she could put her head in a deep freeze and stop thinking.

August twenty-third was a scorcher. The heat wave was front-page news.

"I hope that courthouse has air conditioning," Nancy said at breakfast. She was wearing a thin white blouse and a cotton skirt, and she looked very pretty. The judge is going to fall for her, Becky thought dismally.

"I can't find my feathered barrette," Becky said, as she put two spoonfuls of sugar in her coffee.

"You're not going to wear that, are you?" Nancy was appalled.

"Why not? I think it's pretty."

"It's not appropriate."

"You're wearing a frilly blouse."

"That's different."

Stacey giggled. "Nancy would look funny if she was wearing a barrette instead of a blouse. When you come home, Becky, are you going to be that, whatever-you-call-it minor?"

"I don't know if we'll get an answer right away. I doubt it."

But in a few hours she would have some idea of the result. What if she lost? All the time she'd been thinking about becoming legally independent she hadn't given much thought to the possibility that she might not win her case. It had seemed so obvious to her that she should be on her own, and after her visit to the hos-

154

pital she was quite sure her mother would not be coming home. She didn't want to think about her mother today. Even if Mrs. Jones were well, Becky didn't think she would understand what she was doing. Her father would, though. She knew he would be proud of his daughter for wanting to take care of herself.

She found her feathered barrette on the living-room sofa, put it on, and then took it off. It looked crazy with her tailored blouse and denim skirt. Becky wondered if she looked like someone who could take care of herself.

"I shouldn't be riding with you two," Becky said to David and Nancy in the car. The county courthouse was about three-quarters of an hour away from home.

"Why not?" Nancy asked, turning around in her seat next to David, who was driving.

"I don't think people go to court with someone from the opposite side."

"We're not your enemies," Nancy said. No comment, Becky thought to herself.

Mr. Bracioli was there when she arrived and introduced her to a social worker attached to the juvenile court. Mrs. Bauman was a middle-aged woman with hair dyed pitch-black and a worried expression on her rouged face. She was dressed very smartly in a black linen suit, and Becky thought she looked out of place in the dingy hall of the courthouse where they were waiting. "Mrs. Bauman went to see your mother," Mr. Bracioli said in a low voice to Becky. "She doesn't think your mother will be able to function as a parent."

"I know. I went to see her too." She too kept her

155

voice low. "I suppose that should help me, shouldn't it?" Becky was aware that her words sounded all wrong. "You know what I mean?" she added, embarrassed.

"Yes, I do."

They had rather a long wait before the group was ushered into a private room where the judge was sitting at a long table. Judge Stanley was a large man with a long, owllike face who peered out at the world over his gold-rimmed glasses. He and the table looked too large for the room they were in. He motioned them all to sit down. At a small table off to one side was a court clerk, who would take down everything that was said.

Becky's heart was beating so rapidly she thought it was going to burst. She sat down next to Mr. Bracioli, while Nancy and David settled themselves across the aisle. She threw nervous glances at Nancy, whose face was set in a grim, tight line. Her sister stared straight ahead, avoiding Becky's eyes.

"I would like to call on my client first, Your Honor, if I may." Richard Bracioli stood up to address the judge.

The judge made a gesture indicating that he should go ahead.

Mr. Bracioli motioned to Becky to stand and approach the judge's table. Then he addressed her. "Your full name?"

"Becky, Rebecca Jones." She spoke in a clear, quiet voice.

"Your age?"

"Sixteen."

"You live in Dorchester?"

156

"Yes, sir."

"With whom are you living now?"

"My two sisters, Nancy and Stacey."

"And your parents?"

"My father is dead, he was killed in an accident, and my mother is in a mental hospital."

"I would like you to tell the judge in your own words why you have petitioned the court to become an emancipated minor." The judge then told her to sit down and relax.

She smiled nervously. The idea of relaxing was ridiculous. But she sat down in the narrow chair and glanced at the judge. His eyes were half closed and she wondered if he was listening. She thought a few minutes before she spoke. "As I have said I have no parents at home, and so I feel I have to be on my own more or less anyway. As I see it, since I am now considered a minor, either my older sister will become my guardian or adopt me, or I'll become a ward of the state. Or I can be emancipated. The last is what I want. I feel I can take care of myself. I've got a job, I can support myself, and if we get money from my father's accident I would be entitled to my share."

"Is that one of your reasons, to get your share of the money from any settlement made on account of your father's accident?" The judge shot the question at her and she saw that under his droopy eyelids his eyes were shrewd and alert.

"Why no, that's not my reason, sir. But I think I would be entitled to it. But it's not the money I'm after," she said indignantly.

"You'd get your money no matter what," Nancy cut in angrily. "I don't want your money."

157

"I never said you did. I just wanted to show I'll be able to take care of myself financially."

"You're the one who said you hated that money," Nancy said bitterly.

"I couldn't put it to a better use," Becky answered tartly. "Dad would be glad. He'd be proud of me."

The judge was watching the two of them from under his narrowed eyes. "You girls don't get along very well, do you."

"We get along pretty well. We would if we weren't living together," Becky said.

"You mean if you got your own way all the time. Sure Dad would be proud of you. He was always proud of you. As far as he was concerned, he had only one daughter." Nancy blew her nose into a tissue.

"That's not fair," Becky yelled. "He . . ."

The judge stopped her. "No more of this. Let's get on with the business at hand. No more emotional scenes, please." He went on to ask Becky more specific questions about her job and how much she earned.

But his calm manner could not dispel the tension in the air. Becky was sure she could feel waves of hostility coming from Nancy. It felt as real as if little daggers were flying across to pierce her skin.

"Have you ever been in any trouble? Been arrested for anything?" The judge addressed Becky.

"No, sir, never."

"What about your schooling? Have you a high-school diploma?"

"No, not yet. I would like to go on with school. If I get some money I can. If not, I suppose I'd have to work full time and go back to school later."

"It's been my experience that very few young

158

people go back to school once they quit." The judge picked up a pencil and doodled on a piece of paper.

"I would do it," Becky said bravely. "When I make up my mind to do something I do it."

Mr. Bracioli interrupted here. "Your Honor, I have good reason to believe there will be some settlement from the insurance company so that Becky will be entitled to some money, and she would continue her schooling."

"Or she might just spend the money on a car or something else. If she were emancipated she would be free to do what she wanted. What makes you think she would be prudent?" The judge hardly looked up from his doodle paper when he spoke.

Becky looked to Mr. Bracioli. She didn't know if she was supposed to try to answer that or not. Mr. Bracioli merely shrugged and said, "I don't know how we can prove how she would behave, but I believe she is a responsible young woman."

"That's what you think," Nancy cut in. "She doesn't know anything about handling money, she's told me that herself. If she gets into debt or trouble, I'll still have to bail her out."

"No, you won't. You won't have to do a thing for me." Becky's voice choked up.

"That's what you say now. . . ."

The judge put up his hand to silence them. "You'll have your chance to speak," he said to Nancy, "but let's have some order. This is a courtroom, not a boxing ring. What are your objections to your sister's leaving home?" he asked her.

"I think it's a crazy idea," Nancy said vehemently. "She has a good home, everything she needs and wants.

159

I think it's just one of her scatterbrained ideas. She's going through all this rigmarole, and in a few weeks she'll come back wishing she was home again. She's putting everyone to all this trouble for nothing." ·

Becky was so furious she started up out of her chair and only sat down again when Mr. Bracioli put a restraining hand on her arm. "That's the most outrageous thing I every heard. I'll never come home again. I can't wait to get out of that trap. You're jealous, that's all; it has nothing to do with me or with the kind of person I am."

Nancy sat down in her chair trying to hold back the indignation that would make her cry. "Sure I was jealous, I had good reason to be. She was always our father's darling—he never paid any attention to me. I was always left home with my mother while they went off on their hikes or to pick their precious mushrooms. I was always helping my mother."

"You could have come," Becky said, trying to control her own voice. "You never wanted to. You said it was boring. Don't blame Dad now. That's not fair."

"Let's not dig up the past," the judge said gruffly. "Just tell me briefly why you think your sister wants to be emancipated."

It took Nancy a few minutes to speak more calmly. Then she continued. "She says she wants to be independent, whatever that means."

"Don't you think she doesn't want you to be her guardian?"

"I'm sure she doesn't." Her voice was still choked.

"What about you?" He glanced at a paper in front of him. "You're just barely nineteen yourself. Why do you want to take on the guardianship of a girl old enough to get into trouble and who you think can't take care of herself? What control would you have over her?"

"I think it's my duty, sir. She's my sister." Nancy sat with her hands tightly folded in her lap.

The judge sighed. "Your duty. Do you care for your sister?"

"Yes, of course I do. We're a close family."

"But you don't trust her, is that it?"

"I don't think she's old enough to take care of herself," Nancy repeated firmly.

"But you consider yourself old enough to take care of a sixteen-year-old and a nine-year-old? Isn't that a big load for you?" The judge went back to his doodling.

"I've been doing it," Nancy said.

"You haven't answered my question. How would you control her?"

Nancy's mouth tightened. "I don't know, Your Honor."

Becky was dying to say something and kept trying to get the judge's eye. But he turned to the social worker. "I understand you went to see Mrs. Jones, the girls' mother. How did you find her? Will she be able to return home and function as a parent?"

"No, sir. I doubt that she ever will. I have the doctor's report, which states that the prognosis is not good." She handed the clerk a sheet of paper.

Judge Stanley looked up from his scratch pad and glanced from one sister to the other. "Anyone else have anything else to say?"

"I do," Becky said in a soft voice. "My sister and I do

not get along. We should not be living in the same house. I don't think it's fair for a sister just a few years older to tell you what to do all the time. She is very bossy."

"You need to be told what to do," Nancy said sharply.

"That's what you think. You want control."

The girls were glaring at each other. Becky felt a wild desire to strike out. She wondered if she would have hit her sister had they not been in a courtroom. Then Becky turned to the judge and the tears were streaming down her cheeks. "I came here for help, please help me. I've got to be on my own. It's not just because of her, I swear it isn't. She always gets me into this trap. I don't think we hate each other as much as it sounds; we're just different. Terribly different. I need to be on my own, I need to be alone. I can take care of myself, I know I can. We'll get along fine if I'm treated as an equal, not a baby. With our parents gone there's no sense to my living at home. Please understand. Please give me a chance."

Awkwardly, Mr. Bracioli put his arm around her. "Take it easy, Becky."

She was still crying softly when the judge said that the court would reserve judgment and let the attorneys know the decision soon. "Bring in the next case," he said.

Outside the courthouse Becky asked Mr. Bracioli to take her home. "You can ride with us," Nancy said. "You're being childish."

"If you say or imply that one more time, I'm going to scream. Yes, I know I can ride with you, but I don't feel like it. I don't suppose you can understand that."

David took hold of Nancy's arm and asked the other lawyer if it was convenient for him to take Becky home.

"Yes, sure." Mr. Bracioli led Becky to his car.

"I suppose I made a fool of myself," Becky said, sitting beside her lawyer. "Crying that way."

"You did all right. You said what you had to say."

"What do you think will happen?"

"I think your chances are pretty good. I hope so."

"I hope so too." Becky thought about how awful it would be if she failed. Living with Nancy after all this would be unbearable. She didn't want to think about that; she had to win.

"What do you think the judge will say?" she persisted.

"I think he saw pretty clearly that you and your sister don't get along, and that living with her is not constructive for you. He has to base his decision on what he thinks is best for you. It is not just a question of whether you are mature now or not—obviously a sixteen-year-old girl is not necessarily mature. He must decide whether you are living in a situation at home that will allow you to develop into a self-reliant young woman or in one that is keeping you back. I think he will find you will be better off on your own under the circumstances."

"I hope so," Becky said again with a deep sigh.

14

Becky wrapped the loaf of warm banana bread carefully in silver foil. She could feel Nancy's eyes watching her as her sister ate breakfast. "I'm taking it to Mr. Kowalski," she said over her shoulder. Despite Nancy's silence she added, "He's been so nice, letting me take so much time off."

"Do you intend to keep that job if you get your okay from the judge?" Nancy asked.

"Sure. I like it."

Nancy put her cup down heavily. "I hate it, I hate what you're doing. I don't mean the job alone. . . . "

Becky swung around. "I wish you didn't. It makes me feel that you hate me."

"It's hard to separate the two." Then in a pleading voice, Nancy said, "I wish you'd give up this whole emancipation idea."

"I'm not going to. I wish you'd give up trying to make me. I thought we could be friends."

"We're sisters, not friends."

"Can't we be both? Or don't you want to be friends?"

164

Nancy didn't answer. She put her breakfast dishes in the sink and picked up her pocketbook. "See you tonight," she said, and left.

Becky felt depressed when she got to the coffee shop. She gave Mr. K. the loaf she had baked, and even his genuine pleasure did not cheer her up. Her feelings about him, she realized, were as uncertain as everything else in her life right then. She didn't want anyone to love her. She liked him a lot but didn't want to get too close. In the same way, she was holding Tim off. Her drive to be alone came from a deep need to regroup her strength against her losses. She had thought about it on the walk over. When she asked Nancy if they couldn't be friends as well as sisters, she realized she was asking for a closeness that she herself couldn't give. She wondered if she would ever be able to love anyone again, wholly and freely, without the fear of losing them the way she'd lost her father and her mother.

"What's the matter?" Mr. Kowalski asked. "You look like you've lost your last friend."

"Maybe I have," Becky said.

"Don't worry, you still got me. I'm an old man, but I'm also a good friend. Maybe if I showed you an apartment you'd cheer up?" He looked at her slyly.

"You bet." She pulled her mouth into a wide grin with her hands. "See?"

"Come on. It's slow. We'll close up for a few minutes and I'll show you."

She felt both excited and nervous. Would she really be able to do it? She hadn't given much thought to the details—an apartment, furnishing it, signing a lease. They had been words she had said glibly; but suddenly

Mr. Kowalski had given them meaning. A real apartment. Being alone. Making a decision. Choosing where to live. She had never bought a piece of furniture in her life. She had never bought dishes or pots and pans. These were things you thought about when you got older, when you got married. Was she crazy to want to become older so quickly?

"Come on." Mr. Kowalski had on his jacket and was at the door. "I'll put up the sign "Be back in ten minutes." No one will know which ten minutes." He chuckled and held the door open for her.

Becky followed him into the street, across an avenue, and down a few blocks. She looked at the neighborhood with a new interest: If she lived here she could market in that store, buy candy in that little stationery store. It was a tiny village of its own—a complete little neighborhood with kids playing ball in the street and people in their yard cleaning up their flower beds. Becky felt an almost proprietory feeling when she saw a young man painting his front porch, and returned the smile he gave her. Mr. Kowalski stopped in front of a three-story rambling gray house that needed a paint job, with a wide veranda running across its width. It had been an elegant one-family house at one time, but now it had been turned into an apartment building and was rundown. An outside stairway going up the side did not add to its beauty.

"My wife and I lived here for twenty years," Mr. Kowalski said, opening a door at the rear of the hall into a bright, sunny kitchen. "Now I live here by myself. Five years since she passed on." He showed Becky his living room and a small dining room, and discreetly pointed to a door that he said was the bedroom.

166

"Did you live in the whole house when your wife was with you?" Becky asked.

"Oh, no. First it was a two-family house, that's when we bought it. Then my wife thought we should make more apartments. Now there are five—two on this floor, two upstairs, and one on the top floor, which is only half the house. That's the one I want to show you. You like this?"

"Oh, yes, your apartment's great." She looked up at the high ceilings and the fireplace. "Does the one upstairs have a fireplace too?" she asked eagerly. "This must have been a beautiful house once."

"I guess so," he said indifferently. "I don't care about the past the way some old people do. It's today that counts." He took her back into the hall, led her up the two flights of stairs, and knocked on the door at the top landing. "Mrs. Goldberg? It's me, Mr. Kowalski. I'd like to show the apartment if you don't mind."

A thin, little voice answered, "Just a minute, just a minute. . . ." Shortly, the door opened and Mrs. Goldberg greeted them. She was a small, birdlike woman in a neat housedress and with a pile of beautiful white hair carefully arranged in coils on top of her head. "I haven't cleaned yet, but you're welcome to come in."

Mr. Kowalski introduced Becky. With one glance at the spotless apartment, she knew it had to be hers and that she would move heaven and earth to get it. The rooms were small, but the ceilings were high, as they were downstairs. The sun poured in, there was a fireplace, and, best of all, the living room was enlarged by a window seat set deeply into a semicircular set of windows.

"I love it, I love it," Becky said. Then her face fell. "I suppose you're moving pretty soon?" she asked Mrs. Goldberg.

"The end of the month. I'm going to California to live with my daughter." She looked around her room sadly. "I don't like to go, but she thinks I shouldn't live alone anymore. Because of my eyes, I don't see so good now. I don't know . . . but I don't like her to worry about me."

"You'll probably like California," Becky said politely. "Your apartment's beautiful, I love it. But I may not be ready to move for a while. It probably won't be vacant by the time I could take it. Anyway, thank you for letting me see it."

Out in the street again, Becky said in a dismal voice, "I wish I hadn't seen it. The judge may take weeks to give his answer."

"If you want something bad enough, you get it. Most of the time anyway."

"Did you always get what you wanted?"

"Not always. But I wanted my wife and I got her. I really chased after her," he said with a chuckle. "I never cared much about money, but I should have had a profession. That's where I missed. I always said I'd go back to school but I never did. It seemed out of my reach, but I could have done it. Yep, I could have."

Mr. Kowalski unlocked the door of the store and took down the sign. "They're not standing in line waiting to get in," he said drily.

"I suppose you're going to rent the apartment as soon as you can," Becky said.

"We'll see what happens." That was as much of an answer as she could get from him.

168

*   *   *

When Becky came home from work she found the
house filled with flowers. She could smell the roses before she came in the door. "What's going on?" Both
her sisters were in the kitchen.

"Nancy's getting married," Stacey said, "and I'm
going to be a bridesmaid. I'm going to carry the ring."

"You're getting married now, tonight?"

"No, of course not." Nancy had her sleeves rolled up
and her dress was covered with a large apron. She was
rolling a pie dough to a paper thinness. "But I told
David that I'd marry him. He went off the deep end."
She motioned to the dozens of roses.

"How wonderful." Becky threw her arms around
Nancy. "I knew you'd eventually say yes."

"Of course. I knew that too. But you know me, I
have to go through all the negative reasons first. Look
out, you'll get flour over everything," Nancy said, but
she returned Becky's enthusiastic embraces.

"I don't care. I'm so happy."

"Is David coming over?" Stacey asked.

"Yes, later. We're going to call his mother in Ore-
gon."

"I never knew he had a mother," Becky said.

"Everyone has a mother," Stacey told her.

"Have you set a date?" Becky asked.

"Not definitely. David wanted me to tell him before
we knew about the settlement. He said otherwise I'd
accuse him of marrying me for my money." Nancy
laughed. "He'd be just the one to do that."

"What about the settlement?"

"We should hear any time now. David is expecting
an offer from them."

169

Becky thought about the apartment, but she decided not to say anything until she knew she could take it.

Later in the evening Becky still had her light on when Nancy came upstairs to go to bed. She called Nancy into her room. "Are you going to tell Mom you're getting married?" she asked.

Nancy sat down on her bed. "I guess I will. But I don't suppose it will mean anything to her. It's hard to believe that she doesn't understand." She stood up to say good night and then bent down to kiss Becky. "I thought we'd be closer, after all that has happened. I thought tragedies brought people together."

"We can be close. Now with your getting married it will be so much better if I live separately."

"David and I would be happy to have you live with us."

"I know." Becky sighed. "Tragedies also make you think a lot. How accidental everything is. I think the only way we'll ever be close is when we're on an equal footing. We could never be that if you were my guardian." Nancy didn't answer.

Becky looked at her sister's firm mouth and thought, I'll never prove anything by talking to her. Maybe someday if I show that I'm okay alone she'll understand.

She said good night and asked Nancy to switch off the light so that she could go to sleep.

15

A few days later they were summoned to David's office to discuss a settlement offer. On her way there Becky stopped to look again at the chair with the heart-shaped back. This time she went inside the store to get the price and was shocked to learn it was forty-nine dollars and ninety-five cents. "That's fifty dollars," she said to the salesman.

"It's a well-made, sturdy chair. Not one of the cheap wicker kind."

"Can I leave a deposit on it?"

"Sure. How much do you want to leave? I suppose you want your mother to come in to look at it." He gave her a knowing smile.

"No, I don't want my mother to come in to look at it," she said briskly. She was wearing her high-heeled sandals and had pinned up her hair against the heat, and thought the salesman was an idiot. "Will five dollars hold it?" She took a bill out of her purse.

"I guess so," he said indifferently. "I'll give you a receipt."

Becky walked out of the air-conditioned store into the early September heat, highly pleased with herself. Maybe it was unlucky to buy something before she knew for sure about her future, but she had decided to put such childish omens behind her.

Nancy and Stacey were already in David's office and the three of them were waiting for her. She did not tell them why she was late.

"We've got an offer from their lawyers and it's up to you three to decide whether to take it or not."

"How much?" Becky asked. She was sitting between Nancy and Stacey, all three facing David behind his desk.

"Two hundred thousand," David said. "Don't forget our office takes a percentage. I think I can persuade Mr. Timmins to take twenty-five percent instead of the usual thirty or forty. That leaves a hundred and fifty thousand. What do you think?" He looked from one to the other.

"I can't imagine that much money," Stacey said. "The most I ever had was fifty-three dollars and seventy-five cents in the bank."

"What do you think?" Nancy asked David.

"I'd like you three to make up your minds. We could hold out for more, but I don't know if we'd get it. They say this is their absolute best offer. But they always say that. It's not a bad settlement. You see, the Connecticut law says a settlement is made based on your father's assets at the time of his death, not on his potential lifetime earnings as it is in some other states. His assets weren't that high; most of it is in your house. On that basis two hundred thousand is fairly generous."

"We'd each have fifty thousand dollars," Becky said.

172

"I've spoken with the social worker at the hospital. As long as your mother is there, the workmen's compensation and her widow's benefits will take care of her. If she leaves, she'd have that income and we all would be responsible for supplementing it if necessary." David grinned. "I'd be a member of the family by then. I think she'd be well taken care of."

"I think we should take it," Becky said. "My vote is yes."

"I don't want to be in a hurry," Nancy said. "Can we think about it?"

"Of course. Think about it as much as you want."

Becky slipped her feet out of her sandals. She loved high heels but she had walked too much in them. Like Stacey, she couldn't imagine having fifty thousand dollars.

"If we invested the money at even ten percent, you'd each have an income of around five thousand a year," David said.

"You think we should take it?" Nancy looked to him for an answer.

"I want you to decide. You can take a chance and try to get more, but they might even come back with less. That's happened."

"Let's take it, then. It sounds good to me." Becky tried not to sound urgent. She felt that the more she said yes, the more Nancy would cautiously say no.

"Let's think about it overnight," Nancy said.

That evening Becky left Nancy alone to do her thinking. She said she was going to the movies with Tim. "He'll be leaving for school soon, and we want to see each other as much as we can."

"Shouldn't we discuss the money?"

"What's there to talk about? We just keep saying the same things over again. You know how I feel and you heard what David said. I say let's take the money."

"It's a big decision."

"Talking about it isn't going to help. I say take it; if we say no we could end up with less. Now you have to decide. See you later."

On the way to the movies, Becky told Tim about the apartment. After the show, he pulled the car onto a dirt road and stopped in a side clearing. He leaned back and put his arm around Becky's shoulders. "You're not going to be stingy with that apartment, are you? Will you let me come up and cook some meals for you?"

"Sure." She was silent for a few minutes. "But I don't want to get involved, Tim. Let's get that straight. I mean, being alone and all that is going to be tempting. There's no one going to be around to stop me or tell me it's time to say good night and go to bed. Alone. I don't want to get started. I'm sitting on a lot of emotions; and until I really know where I'm at, until I know where I'm going and that I'm in full control, I want to go it alone. I like you a lot, Tim, but please don't make it hard for me. Besides, you'll be going away. We're going off in different directions."

"Yes, I know. I feel this is kind of the end of something for both of us. But I hope not the end of our being friends."

"It doesn't have to be. It's a beginning too. Don't you think so?" She looked at him expectantly.

"I sure do. Exciting. I suppose I feel the same way as you do, about getting involved. Don't misunderstand me. I like to fool around with girls, but I don't want to

174

get involved. With you I could. But you can give me a kiss. . . ." He turned her face to him and bent down to meet her lips. They kissed each other for a long time.

When they finally parted, Becky was laughing. "If this is your idea of making it easy . . ."

"Did I say I was going to do that?" Tim was laughing too. "You've got to help, you know. Don't be so kissable."

"I think we should go home," Becky said.

"Yeah, I suppose." He made no move to start the car and remained turned in his seat looking at her. "Do you think we'll know each other a year from now?" he asked suddenly.

"If we want to we will. There's nothing to stop us."

Tim leaned over and took her in his arms again. When he finished kissing her, he sat up primly in his seat and combed his hair, but his eyes were smiling. "A year's not such a long time."

"Not if we accomplish what we want," Becky said. Suddenly she leaned out of the car and yelled into the darkness, "Yeh, yeh, we're on our way!"

"I'll let you know tonight what I decide," Nancy said the next morning.

"That's not fair to keep us in suspense all day. That's mean." Becky's eyes blazed.

"Well, that's how it is," Nancy said, and left for work.

Becky watched her sister get into the car and drive away. She was banging around the kitchen when Stacey came downstairs.

"What's the matter with you?" Stacey still looked sleepy.

"Nothing."

"You had a fight with Nancy."

"Not really, but she gives me a pain."

Stacey ran over to her and put her arms around her. "Can I come stay overnight with you when you move away?"

"*If* I move, if Nancy ever makes up her mind. Of course you can stay with me, any time. But you'll have fun here with Nancy and David." Becky held her tight. "She's different with you."

Becky was jumpy all day. "Can a person live on five thousand dollars a year?" she asked Mr. Kowalski.

"Lots of people do. But it's not much these days. Depends on how and where you live."

"With the job I'd have more," she said, thinking aloud. Her boss was too discreet to ask questions, but she explained to him what she was talking about. "I didn't even ask you how much the rent was," she said as an afterthought.

"Maybe a hundred and thirty-five a month. Could you manage that?"

"That's not much. Nancy told me rents around our area were a lot more." She looked at him suspiciously. "I don't want special favors."

"Don't worry, business is business. It's the top floor, and I like having one person, not a family, someone I know. But no wild parties, no boyfriends overnight, no hanky-panky."

Becky laughed. "Hanky-panky, that's neat."

That evening Becky sat with a pad and pencil figuring: $135 a month rent. Food. Telephone. Spending money. Clothes. "How much will it cost me to eat a month?" she asked Nancy. "A hundred dollars?"

"You could manage on that. You're assuming you're all set. That we'll take the offer and you'll get your okay from the judge?"

"I'm just planning," Becky said. "We will take the offer, won't we?" Becky's heart was racing. Suddenly she knew why Nancy was so hesitant to give her yes; they both knew the money would be Becky's key to freedom.

"Okay, we'll take the offer," Nancy said.

Becky made a gesture to throw her arms around her, but Nancy turned away. "I hope we're doing the right thing," she muttered.

Becky's own elation collapsed. There's never a real win, she thought. She tore up the piece of paper she'd been figuring on and went outside. She was too tired to go up the hill to her tree, and it was getting dark. She sat in the backyard and looked up at the stars. Her whole life was going to change and it was of her own doing. . . . I hope *I'm* doing the right thing. She looked back at the house with its lights on and up at the window of her own room. It was going to be funny leaving their house, not coming home to her sisters and everything that was familiar. Then she stood up and stretched her body. What was the point of getting sentimental when she didn't even know if it was going to happen?

16

The September days were turning brisk, and when Becky walked to work she could smell the wood fires in the houses along the way. She was back to the routine of school and working in the afternoons. And waiting to hear from the judge. Mr. Kowalski said that if she didn't know by the first of October he would have to look for another tenant.

Tim had taken her out to dinner before he left for school. Becky had felt strange the whole time, as if they had already started their separate lives. Tim was full of talk about his dorm room and the classes he would be taking. "It's a fantastic place," he told Becky, "right along the Hudson. You'll have to come visit; you'll love it."

"You will be coming home some weekends, won't you?"

"Of course. You're going to invite me to cook a great meal for you, remember?"

Becky felt sad, as if she was saying good-bye to a

whole period of her life. She knew that when they met again they would have lost the ease that came with being in touch almost daily, even if it had been only a brief telephone conversation. Tim was honest enough to make no promises, promises she didn't want anyway. "I suppose I'll meet girls there. There'll be a lot of them. But I doubt there'll be another Becky," he had added. "You know what I said, 'a girl to remember.'"

"Oh, yes, that girl, what was her name, the one who made me eat some wild mushrooms. . . ." Becky laughed. "You had a lot of courage. Either that or you were crazy."

The evening went off all right, both of them skirting the serious. It was only when they kissed good-bye that Becky let the sadness show. Tim held her tight and said, "Be careful with those mushrooms, and save them for me. They're special, just for us. . . ."

The call from Mr. Bracioli came the last week in September. He told her to meet him at the juvenile court the next morning. He sounded in a hurry, and she didn't ask any questions. She didn't have her driver's license yet and so she had to ask Nancy to take her there. Nancy thought it was funny. "This is too much. I have to lose a morning at work to take you to find out about something I don't want you to do in the first place. It's cuckoo."

"I know. But what can I do?"

"Maybe you can go with Mr. Bracioli. I can take you to his office—that would be easy."

"I didn't think of that." So Becky spent the evening on the phone getting Mr. Bracioli's home number from David and calling him every half hour until she finally reached him at ten o'clock.

He told her to be at his office at nine o'clock in the morning. "You're going to have to handle all these things yourself if you're alone," Nancy said rather gleefully. "You'll find out what it means to think of everything and do everything yourself." She made it sound threatening.

"I'll manage. Your lipstick is smudged," Becky added amiably.

The judge greeted Becky by her first name as if she were an old friend. At first only she and Mr. Bracioli were with him in his private office; then Mrs. Bauman, the social worker, joined them. There was a more relaxed, informal atmosphere than the first time Becky had been there.

"Do you still want to be an emancipated minor?" the judge asked Becky.

"Yes, sir. Very much."

"You've read the statute and you know the responsibilities you're taking on?"

"Yes, sir."

"I understand a financial settlement has been reached. Are you going to be able to handle your money?"

"I think so. I've been doing a lot of figuring."

"Mrs. Bauman has made some inquiries. Do you have anything you want to say?" He turned to her.

Mrs. Bauman looked at some notes in her hand. "Becky's boss, Mr. Kowalski, says she's responsible. He thinks she can take care of herself. And her school principal gave her a satisfactory report."

180

"You went to see them?" Becky was shocked. "No one told me."

"They weren't supposed to," Mrs. Bauman said drily.

"Best of luck to you, Becky. Take care, don't get into any trouble." The judge signed some papers with a flourish and handed them over to Mr. Bracioli. "Let Becky sign hers, give a copy to the clerk outside, and keep one for herself."

Becky walked out of the courthouse holding her official paper in its manila envelope tightly in her hand. "It's real," she said, her eyes shining. "I can't thank you enough. I must owe you money." She turned to Mr. Bracioli.

"You'll get a bill." He grinned. "It won't break you, don't worry about it."

"I'm so excited. I can't believe it's happened." She wanted to do something, even throw her arms around Mr. Bracioli, but she restrained herself. "I can't wait to tell Mr. K. I can take the apartment."

Becky arranged her flowers in the center of the kitchen table where the girls ate their dinner. "It's my celebration," she said to Nancy and Stacey after telling them all her news. "I brought home a fancy dessert too."

"I think I'll put wallpaper in your room," Nancy said while they were eating. "It will make a nice guest room."

"Or a nursery," Becky said with a grin.

"Not for a while. I don't want that old desk, you can take it if you want. I saw a pretty dressing table that would look nice there. . . ."

181

"The bed is mine. You could get a studio bed, it will make the room look bigger." Becky helped herself to salad.

"I thought the bed belonged to the house." Nancy gave Stacey more vegetables.

"Mom bought it for me when I was twelve. Don't you remember? I was crying that I wanted a brass bed, and Mom surprised me. It's mine, Nancy, and I'm taking it with me."

"I'm not going to fight with you about a bed," Nancy said. "But we're not breaking up the household because you're moving out."

"Of course not. I want to get my own things. I can't wait to get into my own place even if I only have one pot," Becky said.

Becky spent the evening with a pad and pencil making a list of all the things she would have to buy. Just putting them down on paper made her feel good. "I'll help you shop for furniture," Nancy offered. "I think you should just buy the essentials to start with. You can add later."

"That's nice of you. Thanks, but . . . " Becky was embarrassed. She didn't want to hurt Nancy's feelings, but she didn't want her sister's help. "I . . ."

"If you don't want me to help you, I won't." Nancy's back to her was as stiff as her voice. "But I do know a little bit about furnishings."

"I know you do. Much more than me. But this is my very first place and I'd like to do it myself. I'll probably make a million mistakes, but they'll be my mistakes."

"Do it any way you want," Nancy said curtly.

Oh, boy, now I've offended her. Becky stared at her list. She had thought of checking it with Nancy to see what she might have left out, but she folded it up instead. She was on her own, so she may as well start now as ever.

On her way to school on the bus the next day, Becky spied a sign for a tag sale tacked onto a tree. It was being held that coming Saturday. "Will you go with me?" she asked Lisa.

Saturday morning the two girls arrived at the sale at ten o'clock. Becky's face fell when she saw the assortment of chipped china, dented pots, and odd bric-a-brac laid out on several card tables. "I don't want that junk," she said. She had a vision of sparkling new pots and pans and pretty dishes. "Let's go in to the Country Kitchen and see what they have."

Lisa had her mother's car, and the girls drove in to New Salem. "This is more like it," Becky said, walking from one shelf to another looking at the lovely china and pottery and bright pots and pans. "Look," she said to Lisa, stopping at a set of red and white pottery dishes. "Only fifteen ninety-five, and it's beautiful."

"I don't think it's for the whole set," Lisa said.

"Of course it is, it's all together. I'll ask."

Becky went up to a white-haired woman behind the counter to inquire. "Oh, yes, it's lovely isn't it?" she said. "It's Elizabeth Donald's pottery. The cup and saucer set is fifteen dollars and ninety-five cents. I'll have to look up what the other dishes are. Would you like a set of four?"

Becky gaped. "Fifteen ninety-five for one cup and saucer. Are you sure?"

The woman laughed. "Yes, I'm sure. We do have some less expensive things. The Jane Hansen pottery, I believe. The cups and saucers are seven ninety-five. Do you want to see those?"

"No, I don't think so. Thank you."

Becky grabbed Lisa's arm and pulled her out of the store. "Wow. Let's go back to the tag sale, maybe I can find a few things."

The tables were almost empty when the girls got back, and Becky ended up with a decrepit chair that Lisa insisted she could re-cover. It wasn't beautiful, but it only cost four dollars.

"I don't even like the chair," Becky wailed, as the girls struggled to get it into the back of Lisa's car.

"It will be fine after you get a new cover on it," Lisa assured her.

"I never covered a chair in my life."

"I don't think it's hard." Lisa gave the chair a strong push, and both girls stood still. They watched a crack in a leg spread. The wooden leg dropped off and fell to the floor of the car. "Well, that's that," Becky said. "Let's take it to the dump. I never want to see it again."

"Maybe we can fix it," Lisa said weakly. "I'm terribly sorry. . . . "

"Forget it. So I lost four dollars. It's only money." Becky was silent on the way to the dump. After they left the chair and its broken leg behind, Becky turned to Lisa and said, "Do you think I'm going to make a fool of myself? Will I fall flat on my face?"

Lisa's face was very serious. "No, I think you're going to be fine. But I think you should remember one thing. Don't buy any broken-down chairs. At least sit on them first."

Becky looked bewildered for a moment and then burst out laughing. "I'll remember that, thanks."

❋ ❋ ❋

184

A week later Becky stood on the street looking up at the house, her house. She could hear the cries of small boys behind her playing catch and then the sudden sharp crack of a truck backfiring. It could be the small truck coming with her possessions: her bed, a carton of dishes and kitchen things she had found at the thrift shop, a suitcase full of clothes, a couple of chairs and a table she had gotten at the Salvation Army, the one precious purchase of the heart-backed wicker chair, her books and stereo, some posters, and a few pictures.

It had been a long journey, and it was difficult to believe that it had begun less than a year before. In distance she was less than two or three miles from where she had. come, and still she didn't know whether she had arrived or not. Her future held so many variables, so many choices, so many unanswered questions. "You're kind of a pioneer," Tim had said. "There aren't many girls who want to do what you are doing. It's chancy."

"Welcome, welcome." Mr. Kowalski came puffing down the block.

"Who's minding the store?" Becky asked.

"I put up the sign. They'll come back later. I wanted to be here when you moved in."

"Thank you." She held the key he had given her tight in her hand. "It's a beautiful house, isn't it?"

He looked as if he was going to say something in disagreement, but changed his mind. "Sure, sure, it's beautiful." But he was looking at her, not the house.

Becky followed him upstairs, to wait for the moving men.

*　*　*

Nancy and David were going to be married on Thanksgiving Day, and Becky decided to have a party on the preceding Saturday. She invited Nancy and David, Stacey, Tim, who would be home for the week, Lisa and her current boyfriend, Ben, and Mr. Kowalski. Eight people including herself. She took Saturday off from work and spent the day marketing and cooking. Lisa had offered to help, but Becky said she wanted to do it herself. She made two trips to carry her groceries home and up the stairs.

The apartment looked a little better than when she had moved in, but in spite of the pillows she had spread around the floor and the odd pieces of fabric Nancy had given her to hang on the walls, it still looked bare. Her beautiful new chair looked lonely. Becky had to make two more trips downstairs and down the block. One was to the florist to buy three chrysanthemums, all she could afford, and a lot of ferns to go with it; the other was to get a bundle of logs to splurge on a fire. Half an hour before her guests were to arrive she flew downstairs again when she remembered to get apple cider and a bottle of wine to toast the bride and groom.

Nancy, David, and Stacey arrived last. "It's like taking an exam," Becky had said earlier to Lisa. "She'll be watching everything I do."

"Why do you care so much what she thinks?" Lisa had her own way of showing disapproval.

"You don't have a sister. You wouldn't understand." Lisa looked unconvinced.

Nancy came in with a round, fat package in her arms. "I brought you a present." She handed the package to Becky. "I hope you like it."

Becky unfolded a small, beautiful handwoven Indian rug, its red, gold, orange, and dark green colors bright against a white background. Becky was stunned. "It's gorgeous."

"Every room needs at least one pretty object in it," Nancy said. "You can build a whole room around it. I thought it would look nice in front of your fireplace."

"It's fantastic." Becky wondered if it was a peace offering. The small rug was beautiful and it did change the room, although its very beauty made the rest of her things look shabbier to her. But maybe it only looked that way to her, she thought, and decided it was not worth dwelling on.

David had been made a junior partner in the law firm, and Nancy was redecorating their house. There was a lot of conversation about hers and David's plans. "I'm going to have a whole new room," Stacey said, "new wallpaper, new bed, new everything. All pink."

"You won't know the old house," Nancy said to Becky. "I'm making your room into a workroom. It's going to be lovely. . . . "

Becky was waiting for the sadness to hit her. She felt that she had stepped out of a pool and the water had closed up, not even showing a ripple of where she had been. Did she feel jealous? Hurt? Left out? Nancy's life was so full, and she was taking Stacey with her. Becky didn't let any feelings show. She calmly looked after the food and served the dinner and smiled at Nancy.

The dinner went well. Nancy praised the oriental chicken and rice, the salad was fresh and crisp, Stacey said the pie was the best she'd ever eaten. But Mr. Kowalski was very quiet. It wasn't until her family left, and Becky sat down on the floor on one of her pillows

187

and asked Tim to put a record on the stereo and another log on the fire, that the whole room seemed to relax. Lisa, also on the floor, put her head against Ben's knees, and Mr. Kowalski lit his cigar.

Becky looked around at her friends. "I think they're going to be very happy," she said.

"What's the matter?" Lisa had watched Becky during the dinner and now saw that her eyes were misty.

"She's not interested in me anymore. She always used to claim she felt so responsible, yet she didn't ask me anything about myself, how I'm getting along."

"Maybe it was because there were other people around," Lisa said sympathetically.

Becky shook her head. "No, I don't think so. She's all wrapped up in her own life, in getting married and in redoing the house. I'm not blaming her; she has a lot to think about. And I'm not complaining, because I'm the one who left, who wanted to be independent. I guess it's just the shock of knowing that. Realizing that Nancy has her life and I have mine, that we really are separate now. That I truly am alone."

"You have us, you have your friends," Tim said. "We care about you."

"I know, I know." Becky stretched out her hand to him gratefully. "I'm not feeling sorry for myself. I suppose Nancy cares about me in her way. I guess I just didn't expect her to be so literal about leaving me alone; but then that's the way she is. I have to stop fantasizing about the closeness of sisters. Sisters are all different."

"You're different, Becky, and especially when your sister isn't around," Tim said. "It's nobody's fault, and there's no right or wrong. You're on edge with her. You

188

want her to leave you alone yet also be a big sister."

"It will get better," Mr. Kowalski said. "You'll see. As you get older these things won't matter so much."

They sat and watched the fire and listened to the music. Becky thought about her parents and Nancy's wedding, and about herself and her friends here in her own place. The three of them, Nancy, Stacey, and herself, had come through the year pretty well, considering. She rolled off her pillow and stretched out, face down, on her new rug. It was warm and soft and thick.

Tim was probably right that she was different when Nancy was around; but her bond to her sisters had nothing to do with their differences, not even with their uneasinesss when they were together. They might drift further apart than they were now, might see each other less often; yet they had something between them that Becky knew could not exist with anyone else. Was it love? was it blood?— she couldn't give it a name, but it was there, to be taken out when needed.

Tim stayed after the others left. They didn't talk much; they just lay in front of the fire, held each other, kissed.

"Can I stay?" Tim asked when Becky looked at the time and saw it was two o'clock in the morning.

"I thought we had settled all that. No, you'd better not." She laughed. "Mr. K. said no boyfriends overnight."

"Is that the only reason?"

"No."

"Are you happy here alone? Are you lonely?"

"Happy? I don't know if I'm happy. That's a tricky word. But I'm glad, and I feel good. No, I'm not lonely."

189

"I'll call you tomorrow," he said, when he kissed her good night. "Let's make the most of this week."

When she closed the door behind Tim she went back to the fire. The dishes in the sink could wait until the morning. Her room looked pretty with the lights out and only the glow of the fireplace cutting through the darkness. It had been a strange and interesting evening, and an important discovery: Nancy didn't make her angry anymore. She had felt a little sad, but that was different that had been saying good-bye to her childhood. Now she had her own life, and she was glad Nancy had hers.

She picked up two small cards she had neatly lettered to replace the hastily scribbled ones she had put downstairs above her mailbox and next to her doorbell. "Becky Jones." Becky Jones, 319 South Street. That was her, a person with an identity and a home of her own. Becky set the cards down, making a mental note to put them in place in the morning. She got undressed in front of the dying fire and in her nightgown opened her arms to the room. It was beautiful, shabby furniture and all. It was hers, it was home. She had never felt less lonely in her life.

Hila Colman was born and grew up in New York City, where she went to Calhoun School. After graduation, she attended Radcliffe College. Before she started writing for herself, she wrote publicity material and ran a book club. Her first story was sold to the *Saturday Evening Post*, and since then her stories and articles have appeared in many periodicals. Some have been dramatized for television. In 1957, she turned to writing books for teen-age girls. One of them, *The Girl From Puerto Rico*, was given a special citation by the Child Study Association of America.

Mrs. Colman lives in Bridgewater, Connecticut, and has two sons.